THE FORTY-DAY GOVERNESS

REGENCY IN COLOR

MERRY FARMER

THE FORTY-DAY GOVERNESS

Copyright ©2022 by Merry Farmer

Cover design by Erin Dameron-Hill (who is completely fabulous)

ASIN: B0B5HFNK72

Paperback: 9798842747771

Click here for a complete list of other works by Merry Farmer.

If you'd like to be the first to learn about when the next books in the series come out and more, please sign up for my newsletter here: http://eepurl. com/RQ-KX

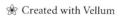 Created with Vellum

CHAPTER 1

KINGSTON, JAMAICA – MAY, 1820

*J*t wasn't the worst possible situation Matthew Weatherly, newly minted Earl of Westbrook, could have found himself in, but it was close.

"...and once again, Lord Westbrook, I am sorry for your loss," Mr. Earnshaw said with an obsequious smile as he shook Matthew's hand, sealing the sale of his deceased brother's plantation.

"Thank you so much, Mr. Earnshaw," Matthew replied with a bow and an uncertain smile. "May you find as much happiness and prosperity with my brother's land as he did."

"Oh, I am quite certain I will, my lord." Earnshaw bowed to him, then turned and marched out of the drawing room where they had finalized the terms of the sale, chuckling to himself as he did.

Matthew watched the man leave with a sense of uncertainty. Had he truly done the right thing in selling his brother's plantation? He'd bent over backwards to make certain

Earnshaw shared his views on abolition and that he would treat the men and women who had worked for his brother with fairness and equanimity, but one could never be certain about such things in the current environment.

And that was without the worry that he was robbing his orphaned nieces, Hibiscus and Heliconia—George's wife had insisted on naming their twin daughters after native flowers of Jamaica as she lay dying after their birth—of their birthright.

"That was a tidy business," George's friend, the Marquess of Quintrell, said, approaching Matthew with a smile. Matthew supposed Quintrell was his friend now as well, seeing as he had so kindly offered his home not only as a place to conduct the business of the sale, but where he and the twins could reside after vacating George's house for the sale months before. "You fetched a remarkable price for the place."

Matthew hummed doubtfully and turned to face Quintrell fully. "But was it enough to provide for Hibby and Helly?" he asked, his brow furrowed and his shoulders tight. "By all rights, it should have been their land and their home."

"Nonsense," Quintrell laughed, gesturing for Matthew to follow him out onto the porch, where one of the dark-skinned house servants was waiting with glasses of refreshing punch for them. "Girls cannot inherit. Your brother's property—here and in England—is yours by right of birth. You are an extraordinary man for considering those girls above your own aims."

Matthew opened his mouth to express that the twins would always be his first concern, and that he had never imagined in his wildest dreams that he would end up with the title and land that had been in his family's possession for centuries.

Quintrell bowled right over him with, "I am quite certain

that those girls are in the very best of hands, after their father's sudden demise, and that they will grow up to be fine young women with large dowries that will make their future husbands quite happy."

Quintrell laughed and slapped Matthew's back just as he began to take a drink of punch. The result was that he spilled a great deal of it down his front.

"Blast," Matthew muttered, searching around for something to dab it away with.

"Kyria," Quintrell called out to a woman who happened to be passing from one of the outbuildings into the main house at the far end of the porch. "Would you be so kind as to fetch something for Lord Westbrook to clean himself up with?"

Matthew's heart fluttered against his ribs as Quintrell brought attention to him. Or perhaps the nervous sensation was because of the no-nonsense look Miss Kingston sent him before saying, "Yes, sir," nodding, then stepping into the house.

There was something about Miss Kyria Kingston that had made Matthew nervous from the moment they'd first met months ago, when he'd arrived on the island. She seemed to be a solid fixture in Quintrell's house, though not as any ordinary sort of servant. She was always impeccably dressed in the very latest fashions and groomed to a degree that would make the ladies of the ton green with jealousy. Miss Kingston was orderliness and organization personified, and even Quintrell's housekeeper seemed to bow to her opinions on the running of the house and everything surrounding it.

Of course, it did not require much of an imagination to determine who Miss Kingston truly was and why she received such favor in Quintrell's house. The resemblance she bore to Quintrell, despite her darker complexion, was striking. Matthew might not have been as world-wise or sophisticated as George and many of his peers were, but he knew enough about the things that were unspoken to guess at Miss Kingston's origins.

"I fear I know nothing at all about being a member of the peerage," Matthew sighed his thoughts aloud as he watched the doorway Miss Kingston had disappeared through.

A moment later, he jerked straight, face heating at his untimely admission.

"I...er...that is, I had no expectations of ever finding myself in the position I am in now," he blundered on, sending Quintrell an apologetic look. "I am the third son, you see," he explained. "George was the oldest, and I always believed that if anything were to happen to him, our brother Henry would have inherited everything."

"Yes, I was sorry to hear of Henry's death as well," Quintrell said. "I knew him through George. He always seemed like a jolly fellow."

"Too jolly, as it turned out," Matthew sighed, feeling a wave of grief. "He never should have attempted to jump that hedge."

And Matthew should never have been saddled with a mountain of responsibilities he was neither educated nor prepared for. He'd always expected to become a scholar or inventor of some sort. Perhaps even a physician. Before George and Henry had died, back when there were no expectations on his shoulders at all, he had filled his days with investigations into all of the latest medical advances that were being made in England and throughout Europe. He'd imagined himself becoming some sort of apprentice to a surgeon in London, or even practicing medicine himself. He'd wished he'd learned more about tropical diseases when word reached him that George had succumbed to a tropical fever all those months ago.

All of that was in the past now. He'd become the Earl of

Westbrook, and the expectations on his shoulder were now of a different sort entirely.

"You are fortunate to have concluded the business of the land sale before your ship departs tomorrow," Quintrell said, gesturing for the attending servant to hand Matthew another glass of punch. "That was cutting it a bit close, wasn't it?"

"It was," Matthew said with a wary look. In fact, he'd been terrified that he wouldn't be able to complete George's business before the *Anthem* set sail for England, and that he would either have to stay another few months in Jamaica— something he was loath to do, knowing how much business awaited him at home in Exeter—or leaving before everything had been settled. He thanked the heavens that he didn't have anything to worry about now.

As if the gods and angels had heard his thoughts and felt it necessary to joke with him, a flurry of noise and movement at the end of the patio caught his attention, and his nieces came tearing toward him.

"Uncle Matthew, Uncle Matthew, is it true we are in danger of being captured by pirates?" Helly asked, her blue eyes wide with horror, as she and Hibby stumbled to a stop on either side of him. They grabbed his hands as if for dear life.

Despite everything, Matthew laughed and his insides filled with light and hope. "Who told you that?" he asked, beaming at the two girls.

"Johnny Marshall told us," Hibby said, her eyes just as wide as Helly's.

"Johnny Marshall?" Matthew glanced to Quintrell in question.

Quintrell laughed. "He's the son of George's plantation manager."

"Oh, I see." Matthew smiled and crouched so that he could be at eye level with the twins. "We shall not be captured by pirates," he told them, trying to sound stern and authoritative, which he was not generally good at. "And if they dare to come near us, I will take up arms…and make certain that you both take them up as well, as you are both far fiercer than I am."

The girls laughed and squealed with delight. So much so that Quintrell winced.

"I think I should carry a sword on the ship," Helly said. "That way the pirates will know to stay away."

"Could I have one too?" Hibby asked. "I should very much like to stab things."

Matthew laughed out loud. His nieces were a bit wild, it was true, but he adored their spirit and rather thought that the three of them would be happy together. They were only just seven years old, but the two of them had been through so much in their young lives, and they were remarkably intelligent for their age. Perhaps that was because George had always valued learning and had hired a governess for them at the earliest possible age.

That governess, Miss Benning, stumbled onto the end of the patio at that moment, as if she had been chasing after the girls and had only just caught up to them.

"No swords for the two of you, I think," Matthew said, rising and resting a hand on each of their heads. They both groaned and complained about that, until Matthew said, "Not until I teach you how to properly fight with a sword."

The twins gasped and lit up at the prospect.

"You would teach us?" Hibby asked.

"Truly?" Helly followed.

"We shall see," Matthew said, smiling amiably as Miss Benning walked stiffly toward them. "Miss Benning might want to teach you herself."

"Miss Benning will do no such thing, my lord," the

governess said, a sharp edge in her voice as she reached their group.

"Oh, dear," Matthew said, sensing the woman's unhappiness and guessing what might happen.

Miss Benning took in a breath and faced him squarely. "My lord, I have thought long and hard about this, and I regret that I have not given you sufficient notice, but I refuse to go to England with you and these—" She snapped her mouth shut rather than continuing, which Matthew thought was likely for the best, judging by the contempt the woman clearly had for his nieces. She took another breath, then said, "I have tried in vain to teach these two hellions manners and decorum, but they are two of the naughtiest, most unmanageable little girls I have ever known."

"Hold on there," Matthew said, handing his new glass of punch back to the servant who had delivered it and pulling his nieces in closer to his sides. "They are young, is all, and they have just been orphaned."

"Yes," Helly said, putting on a decidedly pathetic expression as she hugged Matthew's side. "We have just been orphaned."

Hibby burst into false tears, which Matthew thought was laying it on a bit thick. He understood what Miss Benning meant by calling the girls unruly.

"I am very sorry for their loss, Lord Westbrook, but I cannot continue on as their governess," Miss Benning said. "Particularly as it would mean being confined to close quarters with them for the voyage, which I hear can take up to forty days."

The woman looked as though she would go on and express all her misgivings in a torrent of emotion, but Matthew stopped her.

"I thank you for your service, Miss Benning, and I accept your resignation," he said. "I would just ask that you remain in our service for one day more, until we board the *Anthem*. And, if you would, could you take the girls off to have their tea now while I conclude business here?"

Miss Benning sighed, though Matthew couldn't tell if it was with exasperation or relief. "Yes, my lord," she said, then held her hands out for the twins. "Come along girls."

Once again, the twins whined in protest.

"Do we have to go?" Hibby asked, batting her eyelashes up at him.

Matthew laughed at her manipulations. "Yes, my dears, you do," he said. He leaned over and kissed each of their foreheads. "Go have your tea, then prepare to embark on the journey of your life tomorrow."

That seemed to appease the girls. They squealed and jumped up and down, hugging Matthew tightly.

"Uncle Matthew, you've spilled punch on your nice jacket," Helly said as she stepped away to go with Miss Benning. "You know you mustn't spill things on yourself."

Matthew laughed. "Thank you for informing me, my dear. But see? Miss Kingston is here with a towel so that I can clean up."

The twins seemed satisfied with that and allowed themselves to be led away by Miss Benning.

Miss Kingston stepped forward to offer the small towel. Matthew wasn't certain how long she'd been back on the porch or how much of his interaction with his nieces she'd witnessed, but now that he knew she was there, the fluttery feeling in his gut returned.

"Thank you, Miss Kingston," he said, taking the towel from her with a smile. "You are as efficient as you are—" He stopped. It would have been outrageously improper for him to say she was beautiful, even though she was. Miss Kingston was not the sort of woman to blush and stammer at compliments, though. She was far too serious and commanding for that.

"Thank you for saying so, Lord Westbrook," she said, taking a step back. She met Matthew's eyes without reservation, as if she wasn't intimidated by his title or his nationality, or anything else about him. She was respectful, and Matthew had the impression that she liked him well enough, which was more than she owed to him, if he were being honest with himself.

"You've taken on quite a load with those girls," Quintrell laughed as Matthew did a more thorough job of tidying his jacket.

"They're perfectly lovely, though," he said, smiling.

"They are, but they need a mother." Quintrell nodded. "And you need a countess."

Matthew sighed. "I'm afraid I do." He finished with the towel and handed it back to Miss Kingston with a grateful smile, then turned to Quintrell. "I always assumed I'd marry one day, when I found a woman I fancied. I never had ambitions of marrying for position or to form an alliance of great families. I've always just wanted to be happy in my domestic life."

Quintrell laughed. "I know that feeling, my lord. It is possible for a second marriage, as I have recently come to consider myself."

Miss Kingston stared suddenly at Quintrell, her eyes going wide.

"But not for a man in the position you are in," Quintrell continued. "Mark my words, Westbrook, you need to find yourself a wife of good breeding as quickly as possible. Those girls need supervision and a mother's touch, and you need guidance from a woman well-versed in the *ton* and everything it implies."

"I do," Matthew sighed. "I know absolutely nothing about

the position I find myself in. I need tutelage in all things having to do with society and the aristocracy."

"Lady Irene Sudbury," Quintrell said, as though announcing the woman's arrival at a ball.

"I beg your pardon?" Matthew said, shaking his head and blinking rapidly.

"Lady Irene Sudbury," Quintrell repeated. "I've taken the liberty of perusing the passenger list for the *Anthem*. Lady Irene Sudbury is the widow of the late Earl of Sudbury. Her husband succumbed to the same fever that took George, and she is now returning to her family in England. She is the perfect countess for you as she is already the Countess of Sudbury."

"Oh, I suppose she is," Matthew said.

"She would be able to instruct you in everything you need to know as an earl, and as she is childless herself—she was only married to Sudbury for a year before his demise, you see, and he was nearly twice as old as her—she would be an ideal mother to George's little hellions."

"Yes, I suppose so," Matthew said, rubbing his chin as he considered it. "I have not been introduced to her yet."

Quintrell shrugged. "A minor inconvenience. You will be introduced tomorrow, I am certain, once you are settled on the *Anthem*."

"I suppose you're right." Matthew shifted his stance as another thought struck him. "What I need more immediately than a wife is a governess for the twins," he said. "It is damnably inconvenient that I need to find one on such short notice. I doubt whether I will be able to find a qualified candidate willing to leave everything to set out for England in less than twenty-four hours at all."

"Nonsense," Quintrell said, his smile growing wider. "Miss Kingston will go with you as governess for the girls."

"What is this?" Matthew said, stunned.

"I beg your pardon?" Miss Kingston said at the exact same time.

The two of them exchanged a look as though neither could truly believe what Quintrell had suggested.

Quintrell spread his hands as though he'd made the winning argument in a court case. "You need a competent and reliable governess for the voyage to England," he explained. "Miss Kingston is available, and a daresay she would enjoy exploring life in England, especially with the introductions and support both you and I could give her."

"I have no desire to explore England," Miss Kingston said, speaking to Quintrell in a manner that Matthew found extraordinarily familiar…and further proof of what the connection between the two of them truly was. "I have ambitions here," she said, eyeing Quintrell with particular intensity.

"Now, now, my dear," Quintrell said to her. "Not all of our ambitions can be fulfilled the way we might want them to be. Lord Westbrook is in great need. You would be doing him a service."

Miss Kingston pressed her lips together, let out a breath through her nose, then turned to Matthew with a far softer, kinder look. "It is not that I have no wish to help Lord Westbrook in his time of need—"

"Good," Quintrell said. "That's settled then. I shall have Marian pack your trunk immediately."

"But—"

"The voyage is only forty days, my dear," Quintrell cut her off again. "If you do not like England once you get there, it will be but another forty days for you to return. I will provide you with letters of introduction to my kin in England, not to mention a sizable purse that will help you see to your every need for as long as you are on those foreign shores."

11

Miss Kingston still didn't look certain. She peeked at Matthew for a moment, then frowned at Quintrell. "May I speak to you in private?" she asked, her jaw clenched.

Quintrell sighed. "I suppose so." He gestured for Miss Kingston to follow him into the house. "I will sort this matter for you, Lord Westbrook, never fear. Proceed with your plans for departure."

"I…I will, sir," Matthew told the man with a nod.

He watched as Quintrell and Miss Kingston disappeared into the house, and heard Miss Kingston's low, irritated voice as she spoke, without hearing the words. He hated to engage a governess for the twins who was unwilling, but in the last few months he had observed that the girls liked Miss Kingston. And there was every indication that Miss Kingston would make a fine governess. She was intelligent and brooked no nonsense, which, Matthew had to admit, the girls needed.

Yes, he decided, Miss Kingston would make the perfect governess for the voyage home. And once they reached English shores, he would do whatever he could to ensure she was happy. Perhaps, while he was at it, Miss Kingston might assist him in winning the attention of Lady Sudbury as well, for if there was one thing Matthew knew for certain, it was that he didn't have the slightest idea how to woo a countess.

CHAPTER 2

$\mathcal{I}$t took every bit of the fortitude and grace that Kyria had worked to cultivate in her twenty-two years of life to maintain her decorum as her father suggested she leave her life and her ambitions to become Lord Westbrook's governess and travel to England with him and the girls. No, it hadn't been a suggestion, it had been a command, as if she were one of the servants and could be ordered around without impunity.

"How could you palm me off on a virtual stranger without so much as speaking to me about the matter first?" she whispered to her father as the two of them headed into the house, searching for a quiet room where they could have the spat Kyria knew was coming.

"I have not palmed you off on a stranger," Kyria's father said, his eyes going wide, as if he were genuinely surprised she would say such a thing. "Lord Westbrook has been living in our house these past five months. You knew his brother as well as I did. And you are fond of Lady Hibiscus and Lady Heliconia."

"Yes, yes, I am," Kyria said, trying not to huff and behave

like one of the girls herself. "They are sweet, vibrant creatures, and I would not mind being their governess for a short time at all."

"Then why all this fuss?" her father asked as they settled themselves in one of the smaller parlors that was rarely attended. "One would think you would leap at the opportunity I have presented you with."

Kyria pressed her fingertips to the bridge of her nose, trying to work out how she could best explain to her father— a marquess and a man she could never acknowledge as her sire, even though everyone in the entirety of Jamaica knew it to be true—that his idea of an opportunity was her definition of banishment from all the things she wanted for her life. Her father cared for her, and in private, he treated her like the daughter his legal wife had never been able to give him, but he was excessively stubborn when it came to believing himself to be right about everything.

"My interests lie elsewhere," she said at last, lowering her arm and facing her father with all the regal bearing of a queen. "You have raised me to manage a grand house, to manage *your* house. I know every inch of Spring Garden as well as anyone, and I had always assumed that I would serve as your right hand in managing the place one day."

"And you have always done a remarkable job of it," her father said, taking her hands. He gazed into her eyes with a fondness that Kyria couldn't deny, but with a good deal of condescension as well. "You have the makings of an extraordinary housekeeper, my dear," he said.

"I would like to think that I could be a great deal more than a mere housekeeper," Kyria said, fighting to keep her temper in check. It did get the best of her sometimes, but only because her situation in life was so difficult and awkward.

She was the daughter of a marquess, which should have

made her immensely marriageable and sought after. But she was also the daughter of a woman her father had owned, which guaranteed her nothing in life. Her father was exceptionally kind—not to mention audaciously eccentric—to allow her to live the life she'd lived, but in a way, she wished he hadn't. He'd raised her expectations too high.

Her father sighed and raised her hands to kiss them. "You know I love you, Kyria," he said, "but we must be realistic. You are known widely here. As competent and thorough as you are in your duties to me, all of Kingston society knows the truth."

"That has never mattered before," Kyria said tightly.

"No, and I would not have it matter," her father said. He then winced and went on with, "But I have been in correspondence with a distant cousin of mine, Miss Fairfax, and we have developed an understanding between us."

Kyria held her breath, her insides running hot and cold. She knew precisely what her father was saying, and she knew full well what it meant for her.

"You've engaged to marry her, haven't you," she said.

"I have, my dear," her father confessed. He looked very much as though he were happy about the match, but was trying to keep his joy in check so as not to offend or dishearten her.

Kyria supposed that was the best she could hope for. Except….

"She does not know about me, does she," she said, narrowing her eyes.

Her father hesitated, glancing away, then said, "No, she does not."

Kyria pulled her hands away from his, her heart feeling stung.

"You must understand," her father went on, looking at her once more. "One does not speak of such things in correspondence with a lady. How could I mention you without revealing all?"

They were so few words, but they said so much. If the action wouldn't have been beneath her, Kyria would have crossed her arms, tilted her chin up, and stomped out of the room.

"But all is not lost, my darling," her father went on. "Lord Westbrook's need for a governess on his journey back to England is a boon for us both. We could not have asked for a more fortunate turn of circumstances."

"I do not see how Miss Benning deciding to be a pill and leaving Lord Westbrook in the lurch is a boon for us both," she said.

"It is perfect," her father insisted. "You will be a grand influence on those girls, and on Lord Westbrook himself. His brother's death came as a surprise to him. He is not prepared for the role he must now fill. You could help him as much as the girls."

"I am not a governess," Kyria insisted. "Nor am I a dancing instructor for unexpected peers."

"But you are a competent woman with a deep under-standing of society," her father said. "And your association with Lord Westbrook need only be temporary. Once you are in England, you could achieve all of your dreams and more."

Kyria arched one eyebrow. "I do not see how."

Her father let out a breath, as though impatient with her. "You've a wish to run a grand house, do you not?"

"I do," she said, suspicious.

"Well, what better way to do that than by becoming a housekeeper in a grand country estate in England? Or in one of London's finest homes in Mayfair."

Kyria managed to keep her expression calm, though she bristled inwardly. The idea of managing a house that fine, a house belonging to members of the *ton*, was not entirely unwelcome.

"How do you propose I find myself such a position?" she asked, reluctantly feeling as though her father could be on the right path.

"Lord Westbrook will not be the only member of the nobility traveling home on the *Anthem*," her father said. "Just as you heard me say to Westbrook, the widowed Countess of Sudbury will be on that ship as well. She is young, you know. Only a few years older than you. There was some sort of scandal in her marriage to Sudbury, though I am not aware of the particulars. She is inexperienced, and while Sudbury's brother will inherit the estates and properties belonging to the title, the new earl will, no doubt, set her up with a place of her own. She will need a housekeeper once she is settled. And as the woman will almost certainly remarry, she could very well provide you with the running of one of those grand country estates you enjoy reading about."

Kyria clenched her jaw, fighting to resist her father's scheme. The trouble was that she could see how the entire thing would play out. She very well could work her way into the sort of position she longed for by throwing in her lot with Lady Sudbury. Her father was right about the young countess's future prospects. And many an enterprising woman such as herself had found themselves in a satisfactory position by making themselves indispensable to a member of the peerage.

Kyria let go of her resistance with a heavy breath. "You may have a point," she told her father, not quite willing to admit he was right. There was no need to go encouraging him that way.

"My points are always right," her father said with a wicked wink, as if he knew what she was thinking.

Reluctantly, Kyria smiled. She did love her father, even if he was the most vexatious man in the islands sometimes.

"Now, my dear," he said, taking her hands and kissing them again. "Go ingratiate yourself to Lord Westbrook and his girls. As I said, I will have Marian pack your trunk."

"Yes, Father," Kyria said with a sigh, squeezing her father's hands, then letting him go and taking a step back.

"And who knows?" her father went on as they made their way out of the parlor. "You may find that you like being a governess, and Westbrook may decide to keep you on."

Kyria laughed. "While I enjoy the Weatherby girls, I do not see myself casting aside all my dreams to become a permanent governess. You know where my ambitions lie, Father." She lowered her voice to a whisper at the term as they emerged into the public area of the house.

"Well, if you prove yourself to Westbrook in other ways, who knows what might happen?" her father asked. "He may need a housekeeper of his own. I hear he has inherited several estates and a house in London, and as he implied to me, he has no idea what to do with them."

Kyria hummed, considering it. She supposed it was true that her prospects were broader in England than they were at home. As much as it pained her, she would never find either the acceptance she sought or the sort of position she craved if she stayed in Jamaica. The only thing for it was to accept what possibilities awaited her and to build a life based on those.

She spent the better part of the rest of the day rushing about, paying calls on the few friends she had to inform them of her imminent departure. It was a bit sad to her that she didn't have more calls to pay, but friendship with the natural daughter of a marquess, when far too many people knew how these things happened, was risky for the majority of the women in Kingston. She did have a few companions she promised to write to, which was just enough to make her feel as though she were leaving something behind.

She was still deep in contemplation of all she stood to lose and what she could potentially gain when she nearly ran headlong into Lord Westbrook near the dock in Kingston, after securing her passage on the *Anthem*.

"Miss Kingston," Lord Westbrook greeted her, a surprised smile lighting his face. "I was just on my way to secure passage for you."

"Lord Westbrook." Kyria curtsied to the man. "You've no need. I've just come from the shipping office where I have booked my own passage."

"Oh?" Lord Westbrook looked both startled and impressed. "That was very efficient of you. But then, Lord Quintrell has just finished singing your praises to me and telling me how competent and clever you are. I should have secured passage for you instead of—"

He finished abruptly, turning a bit pink, and looking sweetly bashful.

"I did not mean that as a disparagement, Miss Kingston," he said. "If you feel compelled to manage your own business, I should allow you to do that."

Kyria's first instinct was to find his reaction charming. But she also wondered whether it was strictly proper for an earl to be so easily flustered, as he clearly was.

"I should have allowed you to do it, my lord," she said, inclining her head to him. "I believe I am in your employ now, therefore I should defer to you in these things."

"You do not have to do that," he said, smiling. "I've no idea what I'm doing most of the time."

He immediately winced—another overt reaction that he should have tried to temper…but which Kyria found sweet and appealing.

"I should not have admitted that aloud," he went on, then

sighed. "As you can see, I am a poor employer with a great deal to learn."

Kyria took a risk of being too forward and informal and said, "Lord Quintrell has suggested that I could instruct you in some of the things a new nobleman might need to know, in addition to serving as a governess for your nieces."

Lord Westbrook let out a breath of relief. "I should like that very much," he said. He then laughed suddenly, drawing the attention of a passing fisherman. "Fancy that, needing a governess at my age."

Kyria couldn't help but smile along with his good humor. He was a jolly sort. That might be another way to soften the blow of her entire life as she's imagined it would be being turned on its head. Lord Westbrook would be pleasant company on the ship.

"Are you heading back to Spring Garden?" he asked, hope in his eyes.

"I am." Kyria nodded.

"Then allow me to escort you."

He offered his arm. Kyria hesitated for only a moment. It could be argued that an earl should not escort a woman of uncertain position in such a way. Even if she was the daughter of a marquess. Most of the people observing them would know just how scandalous the gesture was, but by that time tomorrow, they would be out to sea and too far away to care about any gossip.

"You wouldn't happen to know anything about Lady Sudbury, would you?" Lord Westbrook asked after they'd walked in silence for several minutes. He looked pained to ask her.

"I know a little," Kyria said, surprised that he would ask about the woman. "Lord Quintrell believes I should become better acquainted with the countess on our voyage so that she might hire me as a housekeeper once we reach England."

Kyria nearly gasped as the confession passed her lips. She should not be admitting such things aloud to a man she hardly knew.

Except, as her father had pointed out, she did know Lord Westbrook. She'd known him for months. And she'd stood right there as her father had encouraged Lord Westbrook to pursue the young widow's hand in marriage.

"Oh! How convenient." Lord Westbrook smiled. "It seems we have a similar purpose."

Kyria blinked. "Do we?"

"I think so," Lord Westbrook said with a shrug, then continued as though he were speaking to a friend. "You need to convince the countess to hire you for her household, and I need to convince her to make my household hers." He laughed as though he'd told a joke.

Kyria wasn't certain whether to laugh along with him or to blush with embarrassment for his country manners.

"Do you truly intend to pursue the countess?" Kyria asked as delicately as she could.

Lord Westbrook shrugged. "I suppose I should. Lord Quintrell was right when he said the girls need a mother and that I need a countess. The sea voyage would provide the perfect opportunity to court the woman. It is just that…." He let out a sigh.

"Just that?" Kyria prompted him, feeling the slightest bit sorry for the man. He'd lost so much in the last year, and so much was being asked of him. She wished to help him in every way she could.

"It is just that I do not know the woman at all," he finished, looking to her. Appealing to her, really. That was how it felt to Kyria. "How does one court a woman he barely knows with the intent to marry her and make her a mother to his nieces?"

Kyria smiled kindly. A plan was already forming in her mind.

"I believe we could assist each other in achieving our goals, Lord Westbrook," she said. "If you would allow it."

"Yes, please, I would," he said, a bit too eagerly for decorum.

Kyria chose to forgive his lack of propriety. "I could help you woo Lady Sudbury, and perhaps in exchange, you could convince her to hire me as a housekeeper once we arrive in England."

Lord Westbrook's expression brightened. "Yes, I would be delighted to do that, Miss Kingston. From what I have witnessed of your talents while staying with Lord Quintrell, I believe you would make a magnificent housekeeper. I certainly think you will make a fine governess for the girls."

"Thank you for saying so, my lord," Kyria said, smiling.

"Although, by the end of the voyage, I might not want to let you go," Lord Westbrook went on, adding another of his cheery but inappropriate laughs at the end.

Kyria should not have encouraged his informal behavior by laughing with him, but she could not stop herself.

"Who can say?" she asked with a shrug. "If all goes well and we achieve our ends, perhaps you would not be letting me go."

"Oh?" Lord Westbrook asked, a curious light in his eyes and an unmistakable splash of color painting his face.

For some reason his expression made it harder for her to breathe. Or perhaps that was pollen from the stall of flowers they walked past.

"If we both succeed," she explained, pushing aside the odd feeling, "then I will be in Lady Sudbury's employ, but Lady Sudbury would become Lady Westbrook."

"You are right," he said, his smile bright. "I'm sure the girls would like that," he continued. "They are already fond of you, after the time we've all spent living at Spring Garden. It would be lovely not to have to let you go at the end of the voyage."

For the briefest of moments, Lord Westbrook glanced at her, and Kyria's heart seemed to skip a beat. His gaze lingered on her for a moment longer than it should have before he cleared his throat and glanced ahead at the road to Spring Garden.

"Yes," he said, his voice a bit rough. He cleared his throat, then continued, "I think this could turn into a profitable arrangement for us all."

Kyria certainly hoped so. But already, she could feel the ground starting to slip under her feet.

CHAPTER 3

The voyage to England began as well as Matthew could have expected. They had fair weather and calm seas for the first week as the wind carried him and the twins—and Miss Kingston as well, of course—away from the verdant island and off into turquoise seas. He had been anxious that Hibby and Helly would grieve the loss of the only home they'd ever known and the place where both their mother and father were buried, and they were solemn for the first day of the journey, but by the second and third, they were back to their usual, exuberant selves.

"Lady Heliconia, please leave the seagull to its own devices," Miss Kingston gently scolded Helly on the afternoon of the eighth day of the voyage, as she gave the twins a writing lesson on the foredeck. "It does not need you to feed it table scraps to survive."

"But he's been following us since we sailed," Helly argued. "I believe he is lonely and he likes my company."

"And I believe he will grow fat and lazy if you provide him with all his meals," Miss Kingston told her, back straight as she sat on a barrel with a book of some sort in her lap. "If that happens, how will he be able to rejoin his flock?"

Helly let out a loud sigh and tossed the last of the bread she'd kept aside after luncheon to the cheeky seagull.

Before she could say anything, though, Miss Kingston spoke again. "Lady Hibiscus, pray do not vex the ship's cats. They are here to keep mice from the stores, not to be played with."

Matthew glanced across the deck where Miss Kingston was looking to find Hibby with a beleaguered cat in each arm, hugging them far too tightly.

"I like cats," she said, beaming at the two creatures, even though one of them was struggling to get away. The other seemed to have given up and was resigned to its fate.

Matthew could imagine Miss Benning shouting at Hibby and frightening her with every sort of story about how cats were vermin and riddled with fleas, but Miss Kingston merely said, "Tom and Bob will be there when you finish your lesson. Right now, we are learning to write prettily."

Matthew smiled—even more so when Hibby groaned and reluctantly let go of the cats to return to her lesson—because everything about Miss Kingston was pretty, as far as he was concerned. Unlike several of the other female passengers, Miss Kingston looked and behaved as though they were not only still on dry land, but as though they might be called to an audience with the king. Not a single hair was out of place in her delicate style, despite the constant sea breeze. She'd managed to keep her soft blue gown pristine as well. The style and cut flattered her delicate form, and the color made Matthew feel as though she fit perfectly with the marine backdrop.

Which was more than he could say for himself. He hadn't quite tied his neckcloth right that morning, he had an unidentified splotch on his Hessian boots, and bathing and shaving with salt water that morning did not seem to agree with his complexion.

"Do we have to practice handwriting now?" Helly whined, taking up the board she was working on that had a piece of paper tacked to it. "It is too difficult."

"Yes," Hibby agreed. "The ship is moving too much. I cannot keep my lines straight."

"Ah," Miss Kingston said, a knowing smile lighting her face. "That is precisely why we must practice on the ship. If you can maintain fine penmanship with the ship rolling over the waves, then you will write beautifully once you are on dry land."

Matthew raised his eyebrows at that logic. He could easily imagine Miss Kingston managing to write perfectly, despite the ship's pitch and roll. He'd already become used to it himself, and he suspected she had as well, but not everyone had. Not everyone could write out an entire alphabet in neat letters while cutting across the deep blue sea.

Matthew was reminded of that when Lady Sudbury's distressed sigh of, "Lord Westbrook, would you be so kind as to help me to the chair over there," sounded from behind him.

Matthew jerked straight from where he had been leaning against the deck's railing, watching his nieces and their governess. He turned, then immediately headed to the stairs that would take him down to the middeck, where Lady Sudbury was emerging from below.

"Certainly, my lady," Matthew said with a smile, offering his arm as soon as he was on the same level as Lady Sudbury. "Did you enjoy your rest?" he asked as affably as possible.

Lady Sudbury looked him up and down with a slight, distasteful curl of her lip before taking his offered arm and letting him escort her slowly across to where a group of chairs had been set up in the shade of the sails above.

"One could hardly call it a rest, Lord Westbrook," she said with a long-suffering sigh. "Will this incessant rocking never cease?"

Matthew worked his mouth wordlessly for a moment before deeming it wise not to reply. The ocean was never still, and if it was, they would not want that at all. Prior to leaving England for Jamaica, he had read several accounts of sea voyages, and the ones where ships hit a calm in the middle of the ocean were more harrowing than those of violent storms, in his opinion.

"Here we are, Lady Sudbury," he said once they'd reached the chairs and he let go of her arm. "Could I fetch you a drink of something?"

"No! Oh, no," Lady Sudbury said, pressing a hand to her stomach as she sank into the chair. "I've hardly been able to eat a thing since we set out."

Matthew continued to smile at her, but he felt at a complete loss. Quintrell had insisted Lady Sudbury would be the perfect match for him, and he did agree. But the poor woman had been so low since they'd set out from Jamaica. He supposed she was a naturally pretty sort, with blonde hair and hazel eyes. She was slim and petite, and Matthew could imagine her commanding a great deal of attention in a ballroom.

But on the ship, there was something...not quite right about her. She'd taken care with her appearance, he could tell, but the sea breeze didn't seem to agree with her. Her complexion was too pink and piqued, and she seemed out of place, even sitting in the deck chair.

A delighted squeal sounded from the foredeck, causing Matthew to turn back to his nieces. He smiled when he saw that a sheet of Helly's paper had escaped from her board, and she and Hibby were now chasing it around in the breeze. Miss Kingston had set aside her book and stood to join them as well. She was surprisingly lithe and graceful as she reached up to catch the paper as the breeze took it. The way she extended her arm created a lovely line with her body.

Lady Sudbury made a sound of pained disapproval. "Must they make all that noise?" she asked.

Matthew turned back to her and found the woman pressing her fingertips to her temples. His smile faltered.

"They are children, Lady Sudbury," he said. "They've only just turned seven, and they have recently been orphaned. I think they can be allowed a bit of license to enjoy themselves."

Lady Sudbury made another disapproving sound. "I do not like children, Lord Westbrook," she said. "They are noisy, troublesome creatures. That nanny of theirs must do a better job of keeping them from disturbing the other passengers on this ship."

"Miss Kingston is a governess, not a nanny." Matthew frowned, his heart sinking. "Surely, you wish to have children of your own one day, Lady Sudbury," he said.

Lady Sudbury raised her eyes to him as if he'd asked an impertinent question. "If I remarry, that will entirely depend on my husband's whims."

Matthew fought not to wince. He supposed hers was not an unusual way to feel about the subject, but it bothered him that the woman did not have an opinion of her own on the matter.

"I shall go up and tell them to be quieter," he said, bowing slightly to Lady Sudbury.

"Yes, do," Lady Sudbury replied, pressing her fingertips to her temples once more.

Matthew bowed one last time, then walked back to the foredeck. The rogue paper had been caught by the time he reached the spot where the lesson was taking place—and thank heavens, since paper was a valuable commodity in the best of times, and even rarer on a ship—but the writing lesson seemed to have been abandoned in favor of some sort of game that involved tossing shells of some sort into a large coil of thick rope.

"This looks like a jolly endeavor," Matthew said with a smile. "Are lessons over for the day?"

"Uncle Matthew! Uncle Matthew!" Hibby and Helly shouted—likely disturbing Lady Sudbury even more. They abandoned their game to throw themselves against Matthew's sides, clinging to him like barnacles.

"You must play with us," Helly shouted.

"It's quite fun," Hibby said. "I'm the best at it."

"No, I am," Helly protested.

"No, I am!"

Matthew could sense a fight about to break out, but it was stopped by a clattering sound. All three of them turned to find Miss Kingston having just landed a shell square in the middle of the rope. She tossed another one as they watched, and it landed with perfect precision.

"As with everything, my ladies," Miss Kingston said with a sly grin, "practice makes perfect."

She underscored her words by tossing a third shell neatly into the coil of rope.

Hibby and Helly gasped and gazed at Miss Kingston in awe. Matthew had to admit that he was impressed as well. As the girls broke away from him to retrieve shells from the coil, then to cross the deck so they could take another turn at throwing them, Miss Kingston strode gracefully to his side.

"I am impressed, Miss Kingston," Matthew said, smiling at the intriguing woman. "Not just with your skill at throwing seashells, but with the way you've managed to occupy two energetic girls."

Miss Kingston smiled. "Lady Hibiscus and Lady Heliconia are dear creatures," she said, "but they do have an excess of energy that needs to be directed into an activity at all times. I trust you do not mind if some of those activities aren't as instructional or productive as others?"

Matthew laughed and watched as the twins took turns tossing shells, then shouting in celebration over their victories. "I am happy if they are happy," he said simply, turning to smile at Miss Kingston.

She smiled widely in return, and Matthew's insides lurched. He ascribed it to the ship rolling over a particularly large wave…even though the sea didn't seem rougher than it was five minutes before.

"How are your plans proceeding where Lady Sudbury is concerned?" Miss Kingston asked, standing a bit closer to him and lowering her voice.

Matthew let out a breath, his shoulders sagging. He peeked over his shoulder to where Lady Sudbury had reclined in her chair, her eyes closed. "Not well, I'm afraid." He turned back to Miss Kingston with a frown. "I cannot tell if she dislikes me or if adjusting to life at sea is what has her out of sorts."

"I cannot imagine anyone disliking you, my lord," Miss Kingston said.

She seemed suddenly flustered after her statement, though Matthew couldn't imagine why. But she recovered her regal bearing and calm manner quickly.

"Perhaps if she saw that you are aware of her needs and can fulfill them for her," she went on, pressing her lips together in thought at the end.

Matthew was immediately assailed by a dozen utterly inappropriate images of ways to fulfill a woman's needs. Only, it was not Lady Sudbury who came to mind with those thoughts, it was Miss Kingston.

He shook his head to put himself back on the straight and narrow.

"A drink of something, perhaps?" he asked. "A spot of tea to calm her nerves?"

Miss Kingston hummed as she thought and tapped her lips. Matthew was mesmerized by the gesture. "Tea, yes," she said. "But with more sugar than usual. And perhaps the tiniest drop of rum as well to ease her nerves."

"Do you think so?" Matthew asked, his brow shooting up. "Would she not be offended if I corrupted her tea in such a way?"

Miss Kingston sent him a conspiratorial grin. "I overheard Lady Sudbury say last night that she likes a bit of rum now and then, but she is too modest to ask for some from the purser."

"Oh!" Matthew said, smiling. "That is useful to know. I shall get her some immediately. Thank you, Miss Kingston."

He turned to go about his mission, but something made him pause and turn back to the governess. She'd returned her attention to the twins, which gave Matthew a moment to study her in the privacy of his own thoughts. She really was quite something. As soon as he secured his place in Lady Sudbury's affections, he would focus his efforts on having Miss Kingston school him in everything he would need to know to be an effective peer.

It did not take long to have the purser dole out a small ration of rum and to have it mixed in with the tea that had already been brewed for the benefit of the ship's passengers. Once a mug was prepared, Matthew carried it up to the deck and over to where Lady Sudbury was still in repose.

Of course, before he could catch the woman's attention, Hibby and Helly came tearing down from the foredeck to join him.

"What is that, Uncle Matthew?" Helly asked, pointing at the mug.

"Can I have some?" Hibby asked as well.

"No, dear girls," Matthew said with a nervous laugh, glancing between them and Lady Sudbury, then at Miss Kingston as she climbed gracefully down the stairs from the foredeck. "This is special tea for Lady Sudbury."

Lady Sudbury fluttered open her eyes and stared at Matthew with a somewhat sour expression. "I thought I told you that I did not want anything to drink, Lord Westbrook," she said.

Matthew flushed with embarrassment and uncertainty, then moved closer to her chair. Perhaps unfortunately, the girls moved with him.

"I've had this prepared for you especially," he said, presenting the mug to Lady Sudbury. "I've been assured it will calm your nerves and your stomach."

"If you do not want it, I will have it," Hibby said with what Matthew was sure the girl thought was a sweet smile.

Lady Sudbury looked as though she would have keel-hauled Matthew, if she'd been up to it. "No, thank you, my lord," she said in a thin voice. "I only wish to be left alone for the moment."

She flopped against her chair again and rested a hand over her eyes.

Matthew's heart sank. He had no choice but to walk away from the woman, the twins trailing him.

The three of them met Miss Kingston by the stairs to the foredeck.

"Your offering was not received, I take it?" Miss Kingston asked, all kindness and disappointment on his behalf.

"No," Matthew sighed, staring at the mug in his hands.

"I said I would have it," Hibby said with a heavy sigh.

"Go collect your writing things and store them in our cabin and you may have all the tea you'd like," Miss Kingston told them.

To Matthew's shock and amazement, the girls did just as Miss Kingston asked them to as soon as they were asked.

"Will wonders never cease?" he asked in a voice of teasing awe. "They never behave so quickly when I tell them what to do."

Miss Kingston smiled, her eyes sparkling with cleverness. "It is all in the tone one uses to command, my lord, and in consistency when it comes to following up on promises made."

"Yes, Miss Kingston," Matthew said, as if Miss Kingston were his adored governess as well.

A moment later, his spirits deflated as he glanced back to Lady Sudbury. "I do not know what I am doing wrong," he said, then, since there seemed nothing else to do with it, took a drink of the tepid tea-and-rum. He winced at the strength of the alcohol, but it would have been criminal to waste it, so he took another gulp.

"Your heart is set on Lady Sudbury, then?" Miss Kingston asked quietly, clasping her hands demurely in front of her.

Matthew glanced between the women. It wasn't his heart that was set, not at all. He merely saw the logic in wedding a woman like Lady Sudbury. His new position in life required it. If it had been up to him, he would have gone a different way entirely.

"She does not like me," he said rather than answering Miss Kingston's question directly.

Miss Kingston hummed in the no-nonsense way she had, then turned to sweep him with an assessing glance. Matthew had the inescapable feeling that she could see right through his clothes, and even past his skin to his insides.

"Perhaps an adjustment in your appearance might help," Miss Kingston said. "I cannot say I am proud of it, but I will admit to women liking the look of a man first and foremost."

"Oh," Matthew said, slightly disappointed. He glanced

down at his disheveled clothes and scuffed boots. He knew he was not horrible to look at, but he wasn't the dashing sort of figure that, for example, George had been, or even Captain Mercer, who commanded the *Anthem*. He considered himself a bit too solid and a little too tall.

Miss Kingston seemed to have other ideas as she surveyed him. "Would you allow me to instruct you on how to improve your appearance and demeanor, my lord?" she asked.

"Yes, certainly," Matthew answered, smiling broadly again. "I need all the instruction you are willing to give me. I haven't known what to do or how to handle myself since George died."

Miss Kingston smiled kindly at him. "Much has been asked of you in a short time," she said. "But rest assured, I will help you in any way I can."

"Thank you, Miss Kingston," Matthew said, relieved beyond measure. "I place myself in your capable hands."

Even as he said as much, a tiny part of Matthew wondered if he might not be happier staying in those hands instead of pursuing Lady Sudbury, even though the idea was impossible.

CHAPTER 4

*K*yria was struck within a fortnight of setting out from Jamaica at how different the rhythm of life on the sea was. As there was little to do in the way of paying calls or going about any sort of daily business as a passenger, every small task seemed to take on monumental importance. And as there was such limited company, all of whom were confined to such tight quarters, every interaction seemed to take on a heightened significance and value. Right from the start, emotions felt more intense than they would have outside the confines of the *Anthem*, and many of the usual rules of social decorum were bent.

"You must take greater care with your clothing, my lord," Kyria cautioned Lord Westbrook as the two of them, along with Lady Hibiscus and Lady Heliconia, perused the various items of the earl's wardrobe that had remained unpacked for the duration of the voyage in his cabin. "I see you've already spilled something unidentifiable on this jacket, and I would consider it the finest you have available for the captain's supper this evening."

"Yes, Uncle Matthew," Lady Heliconia said, scratching at

the spot with one of her small fingers as they all studied the jacket where it lay on Lord Westbrook's narrow bed. "Why do you spill things so often?"

The twins glanced up at him with furrowed brows.

Kyria had to fight to maintain her composure over the darling, censorious looks.

Lord Westbrook let out a sigh and followed that with an ungrateful shrug. "I am sorry. I suppose I should have a greater care when I am eating or drinking things. My mind simply runs off to other places and ideas, and before I know it, I've forgotten that if I turn my wrist just so, something will spill."

"Oh, Uncle Matthew." Hibiscus shook her head, looking and sounding severely disappointed.

When Lord Westbrook glanced apologetically to her, Kyria's heart danced a jig in her chest. The man truly was an enigma. She had only ever known lords who were haughty and sure of themselves and their position. Lord Westbrook was neither of those. But then, she had ascribed that to the way he'd inherited his title unexpectedly and without preparation.

That sad string of circumstances, combined with the man's affable personality, made her determined to help him rise to the challenge of the position he now found himself in.

"I will see to it that the spot is cleaned out of your jacket right away, my lord," she said, sweeping the jacket off the narrow bed—and truly, she did not know how the man fit in such a confined space, considering how tall he was and how broad his shoulders. "While I'm on my errand, perhaps you and the girls could practice tying your neckcloth in the manner I showed you."

Lord Westbrook sent her a doubtful look. "I still do not understand why a simple knot is insufficient for the occasion."

"You've been invited to the captain's supper, Uncle Matthew," Heliconia scolded him. "It's a very grand event."

"You must look as grand as everyone else," Hibiscus agreed.

"Do I not always look as grand as everyone else?" Lord Westbrook asked with mock offense. He peeked at Kyria and winked to show he was teasing the twins.

Kyria's breath caught, and for the life of her, she couldn't shake the intense feeling away.

"I will return once the spot is out," she said, her voice a little too hoarse, as she turned and hurried through the open doorway to the cramped hall.

It was most certainly the oddities of life aboard a ship in the middle of the ocean, she told herself as she moved quickly along to the stairs that would take her down to a lower deck, where she knew the ship's laundering supplies were kept. She never would have dared to interact so informally with an earl otherwise, and she was certain Lord Westbrook would never have given her a second look, let alone a wink, on land. There was no possibility that they would have been able to be alone in a room together, even with the twins present, without her reputation being damaged either. Her race notwithstanding, she'd had a reputation as a lady of sorts in her father's house, and that would have been ruined if she'd been caught alone with Lord Westbrook.

Kyria was shaken out of her contemplations as the door to one of the cabins flew open just a few feet in front of her and Lady Sudbury moved as if she would step into the hall. At the sight of Kyria, the poor woman yelped with fright.

A moment later, she pressed a hand to her chest and breathed out, "I am terribly sorry, Miss Kingston. My nerves have been so distressed of late. The sea does not agree with me."

"I am sorry, my lady," Kyria said with genuine feeling, dipping into a curtsy.

Her heart sped up for reasons other than her strange affinity toward Lord Westbrook. She was never one to miss an opportunity when it presented itself, and with Lady Sudbury, the woman she sought to employ her once they reached land, right in front of her with needs of some sort, Kyria felt the necessity to act.

"Is there something I could do for you, Lady Sudbury?" she asked. "To make your journey more comfortable?"

Lady Sudbury blinked in thought, stared at Kyria for a moment, then at the jacket she carried. "Is that Lord West-brook's jacket?" she asked.

"It is, my lady," Kyria said. "I am taking it to be cleaned for the captain's supper this evening."

Lady Sudbury's eyes widened. "I have been invited to the same supper. But my ladies' maid, Dora, has been indisposed since we set out and has not had any of my things laundered."

Kyria grasped at the unasked question, bursting into a smile at the chance to prove her worth to the countess. "I would be more than happy to have something washed for you, if you'd like."

Lady Sudbury seemed relieved. "My dear, you are a godsend."

Kyria waited in the hall, feeling proud of her quick thinking and pleased that she would be able to help the countess as the woman stepped back into her cabin. A flash of movement at the end of the corridor caught her eye, and she turned to find that Lord Westbrook had stepped out of his cabin. He must have seen the entire interaction, as he made an encouraging gesture to Kyria and mouthed the words, "Well done."

Kyria grinned back at him and, before she could stop

herself or think better of it, winked at him the way he'd winked at her.

"Here you are, my dear." Lady Sudbury distracted her thoughts as she handed over a small pile of underpinnings and stockings. Kyria's triumphant feeling flattened as the countess went on with, "I've no idea how you will manage to launder it all with so little water to be had, but I've no doubt you will sort it."

"Yes, my lady," Kyria said with a polite curtsy, then turned to walk on.

While positive on the surface, something about the interaction struck Kyria as wrong. She feared Lady Sudbury thought of her more as a washerwoman than a potential housekeeper.

As she reached the stairs, she glanced over her shoulder to see if Lord Westbrook was still watching her. Not only was he, he'd seen her look of disappointment, or so she guessed by the look of sympathy he wore. He smiled all the same, which Kyria found encouraging as she descended to the lower deck.

Laundry aboard a ship was a curious affair that had captured Kyria's interest only a few days after they'd set sail. Of course, all fresh water aboard a ship traversing the length of the ocean was desperately needed for drinking. Not a drop of it could be wasted on washing. That left sea water as the only option for cleaning everything from clothing to the decks to one's person. But sailors were a clever lot, and as she'd discovered, they kept special sorts of soap aboard the ship specifically designed for washing with salt water.

Kyria couldn't, in good conscience, leave Lady Sudbury's underthings to be cleaned by one of the male members of the crew, so while she handed Lord Westbrook's jacket off to a particularly talented seaman who promised he could have the garment looking like new by the time Kyria had finished scrubbing Lady Sudbury's delicates, Kyria used the small washbasin and soap to complete a task she knew was far beneath her.

The trouble was, Lady Sudbury did not think it was beneath her. As she scrubbed the light garments against the washboard, lamenting what the soap would do to her hands, she wracked her brain for ways to raise herself in the countess's estimation.

She did her best with the garments as the crewman worked wonders with Lord Westbrook's jacket, and a scant hour after departing for her errand, Kyria returned to the deck where the passenger cabins were located with Lord Westbrook's jacket over one arm and Lady Sudbury's still-damp underthings draped over her other arm, covered by a towel for modesty.

She was surprised to find Lord Westbrook in the hallway, apparently attempting to engage Lady Sudbury in a conversation of some sort.

"…and it came as quite a shock, I must say," Lord Westbrook was in the middle of saying.

He was all smiles and behaving in a perfectly amiable manner, but he'd forgotten to don a jacket when he left the confines of his cabin, and his hair stood up at odd angles, as if he'd forgotten to brush it.

"Yes, I can see how learning of your brother's death by mail could be a shock," Lady Sudbury said in reply. She fidgeted with a small book in her hands, and her back was straight and tense. She even darted looks up and down the dim, tight corridor, as if looking for ways to escape.

"I am doing my best to live up to the position," Lord Westbrook went on, attempting to reassure the countess. "I'd never imagined there was so much to assuming a title and all that, though."

Lady Sudbury continued her restless search for escape,

and the moment she spotted Kyria approaching, she all but breathed a sigh of relief.

"There you are, Miss Kingston," she said, breaking away from Lord Westbrook and rushing to meet her. "I trust all went well with the—" She nodded to the things in Kyria's arms.

A quick wave of annoyance swept through Kyria. Lady Sudbury was rude to dismiss Lord Westbrook so soundly. The man was doing nothing more than attempting to engage her in polite conversation.

"Yes, my lady," Kyria said, smiling despite her annoyance. She glanced past Lady Sudbury to Lord Westbrook. "Your jacket, my lord."

"Oh. Yes. Thank you, Miss Kingston." Lord Westbrook stepped forward to take his jacket from her outstretched arm. As he did, he sent a quick look to Lady Sudbury and added, "You are as efficient as you are kind, Miss Kingston. In fact, I'd wager you would make the perfect housekeeper to someone of great importance." He peeked rapidly at Lady Sudbury.

Kyria fought to swallow her laughter, grinning at Lord Westbrook as openly as she dared with Lady Sudbury standing right there. His comment was much too on the nose, but he was dear for holding up his end of the bargain and working to help achieve her aim with Lady Sudbury.

Lady Sudbury either didn't notice the comment or found it of no consequence.

"Are the things I gave you to launder not dry?" she asked, frowning slightly at Kyria.

Kyria dragged her grin away from Lord Westbrook and looked more seriously at Lady Sudbury. "No, madam," she said. "They must be hung on a line to dry. I assumed you did not wish them to be on display in public parts of the ship, which leaves your cabin as the most suitable spot for drying."

Lady Sudbury looked horrified at the prospect, but before she could protest, Kyria rushed on with, "I could hang them for you, if Dora is still indisposed."

Lady Sudbury stammered for a moment before saying, "Yes, I suppose that is all there is for it. I shall take my book to the open deck while you manage...this." She made a gesture of slight distaste at Kyria's arm, then moved past her and headed on to the stairs leading abovedeck without another word or look for Lord Westbrook.

Kyria was stunned at the woman's inconsideration, but before she could make up her mind whether to comment on it, Lord Westbrook shrugged and said, "Well, one cannot say I did not try."

"You could do a great deal better, Lord Westbrook," Kyria said, sending him a sympathetic look.

"Yes, I know," Lord Westbrook said with a sigh, shoving his hand through his hair. "I have never been very good at polite conversation with noblewomen, though."

Kyria blinked. On the one hand, she had an idea of how his hair had become so disheveled after witnessing the gesture. On the other, she had meant that he could find a better countess than Lady Sudbury, but he had apparently misunderstood her to mean that he could have done a better job of conversing with the sour lady.

She opened her mouth to correct herself, but before she could get any words out, Hibiscus and Heliconia raced down from the upper deck, causing a clatter that echoed in the hallway, and declared, "There's a whale! There's a whale!" in ecstatic unison.

"Truly?" Lord Westbrook lit up as though he were of an age with the girls. "I want to see it. Come with us, Miss Kingston," he said as he strode down the hall toward the stairs.

Kyria couldn't help but smile at the man's boyish enthusiasm. More than anything in the world, she wanted to go view the whale with him.

"I need to hang Lady Sudbury's things first," she said instead.

"Well, hurry up with that, then join us abovedeck," Lord Westbrook said as he passed her.

The corridor was narrow enough that their bodies brushed in several places as he scooted around her. For reasons Kyria didn't want to think about, she found the sudden contact exciting. In a very particular way. Lord Westbrook had a commanding physical presence, or at least he could have if he had more confidence in himself. He was a powerful man hiding in sheep's clothing.

As soon as he'd passed her and moved his body out of contact with hers, he glanced back. Color splashed his face, and his blue eyes held a brightness that made Kyria catch her breath even more. He hadn't felt the same sense of charge in the air at their contact, had he?

A moment later, Heliconia sighed impatiently and said, "Come along, Uncle Matthew."

The moment of spark between Kyria and Lord Westbrook was gone. He turned away from her and told the girls, "I'm coming, I'm coming."

Kyria burst into another smile as she watched the three of them scramble up to the deck. She, meanwhile, had to forego the pleasures of watching a whale—or perhaps the pleasures of watching Lord Westbrook watching the whale were what she was missing—to enter Lady Sudbury's cabin so that she might hang damp underthings.

She was surprised to find that Lady Sudbury's cabin was occupied once she stepped all the way in.

"You are behaving quite informally with Lord Westbrook," Dora, the indisposed ladies' maid observed from a chair in the corner, where she was sprawled.

Kyria nearly gasped at the discovery of the young woman. She was small and pale—a bit green, actually—and even though she was splayed in the chair with a bucket placed conspicuously to one side, she had enough vibrancy to stare critically at Kyria.

"I am on friendly terms with his lordship," Kyria explained as easily as she could as she set the pile of damp underthings on the bed. "He and his nieces have been living at Spring Garden these last few months as he has settled and sold his late brother's plantation." She searched for some sort of line to string across the cabin so that she could hang the underthings rather than look at Dora.

"I suppose it stands to reason," Dora said with a shaky sigh, leaning her head back against the wall and closing her eyes. "Lady Sudbury says he isn't much better than a farmer on one of his own estates and that they should have passed the title to someone else."

Kyria paused in the middle of arranging Lady Sudbury's underthings, a burst of anger hitting her. "Lord Westbrook may not have expected to inherit the title, but he is an intelligent man who has studied at Oxford, and who intended to make something of himself, independent from his family, before the sadness that led to his inheriting," she said in his defense. She'd learned quite a bit about the man through her father, and through conversation with him in the past fortnight.

Dora made a sound as if she either did not know whether Kyria was telling the truth or if it was of no consequence to her. "Lady Sudbury knows he has his mind set on her, and she is uncertain of him," she said.

Kyria stopped in the middle of what she was doing to stare at the woman. She was grateful Dora had her eyes shut and could not see her staring, or her thoughtful look. It was unsettling that the first emotion to strike her upon hearing that Lady Sudbury was not certain about Lord Westbrook was relief, and perhaps even hope. But that was not what Lord Westbrook wanted. She had sworn to help the man win Lady Sudbury over, and it seemed they were even further behind in that task than she had imagined.

She pushed herself into motion again, stringing the clothesline she'd found in one of the cabin's cupboards across the space. She had become very fond of Lord Westbrook indeed, but she knew full well that any attachment more than that of helpful friend was impossible. Lady Sudbury was the sort of woman an earl married not—

No, she couldn't even think of herself that way in the negative, ruling out the possibility of an attachment. She needed to stay the course with the original plan. The captain's supper was in just a few hours, and she would do everything she could to make Lord Westbrook as appealing to Lady Sudbury as possible, just as she knew her friend would do whatever he could to ensure Lady Sudbury hired her at the end of the journey.

CHAPTER 5

*B*y the time dusk began to settle and that evening's chosen few arrived at the Captain Mercer's cabin for supper, Matthew was beginning to feel that he shouldn't have spent so much time watching the pod of whales that escorted the *Anthem* through a bit of the choppy seas. As he tugged at the sleeves of his newly cleaned jacket and tipped his head this way and that in an attempt to loosen his elaborately tied neckcloth, it occurred to him that he should have spent more time with Miss Kingston, having lessons about how to behave as an earl should.

"Are you certain it was necessary to polish my boots?" he asked Miss Kingston as the two of them headed up to the deck so that they could cross over to the stairs that would take them below to the captain's cabin. "They'll be salty again by the time we make our way there."

Indeed, as had become apparent to all as the afternoon wore on and the skies clouded over, they'd been sailing into some sort of storm. Even now, as a few of the crewmen escorted them across the damp rolling deck, Matthew could see dark clouds on the horizon in front of them and the gray haze of rain in the distance.

"One must always make an effort," Miss Kingston told him, raising her voice to be heard over the bluster of the wind and the activity of the crew as they battened down the hatches, or whatever it was ships' crews did when they were approaching a storm. "Even if that effort is likely to come to naught."

Matthew laughed warily despite himself. Effort that would come to naught was what he felt as though he were expending where Lady Sudbury was concerned. Try as he might, the young widow didn't seem to see him as a potential suitor.

Which was why he'd gone through the extra effort, as directed by Miss Kingston, to make himself look as presentable as possible for the captain's supper. As they ducked down another small flight of stairs to the cabins at the aft of the ship, he paused for a moment to allow Miss Kingston to tidy his appearance. She made quick work of straightening his jacket and brushing the few drops of sea spray that had flown up from the ocean off his shoulders. She even went so far to comb her fingers through his hair to make certain it lay properly.

As she did that, the ship pitched particularly fiercely, throwing her against him. Miss Kingston had been able to keep her balance in the middle of a choppy sea better than nearly anyone else on the *Anthem*, but Matthew found himself needing to catch her, lest she lose her balance completely.

The result was that for one beautiful moment, he held her in his arms. She felt so warm and right there, her hands gripping his jacket for dear life. She glanced up into his eyes as well…with something a little more than gratitude.

Matthew was seized by the mad idea that he should kiss

her. He didn't know where the notion came from, but as it whispered loudly to him, he realized it was not a new idea. Part of him felt as though he should have kissed Miss Kingston much sooner than in that moment.

Before he could act upon those feelings, though, the door to the cabin beside them flew open as the ship rolled again. It clattered noisily against the wall. Accompanying it was the sound of the guests who had already arrived at Captain Mercer's cabin shouting or gasping in alarm as the deck teetered under them.

"Ah, Lord Westbrook, Miss Kingston, you have arrived," Captain Mercer said, striding to the door to beckon Matthew and Miss Kingston to enter. "We were waiting for you to begin, but we shouldn't wait much longer. The storm will be upon us soon."

Matthew let go of Miss Kingston—a bit reluctantly, if he were honest—and preceded her into the room.

"A thousand apologies for my tardiness," Matthew said, nodding to the dozen or so people seated around a long table that took up much of the space in the cabin. "Crossing from the other cabins was a bit of a challenge."

"That is one way to put it," Lord Gossling—a middle-aged viscount who was taking passage home aboard the *Anthem* and who was the highest-ranking gentleman aboard besides Matthew said, his voice rough.

"Thank you for agreeing to assist with the supper, Miss Kingston," Captain Mercer thanked the woman as he shut the cabin door. "Your fortitude impresses me. Several of my own crew have been rendered unfit for duty because of the oncoming storm."

"It is my pleasure to serve, sir," Miss Kingston greeted Captain Mercer's compliment with a slight nod of her head.

It struck Matthew as he glanced back at them that Miss Kingston had more strength and composure than even

Captain Mercer. To look at her, one would be hard-pressed to guess that they were in the middle of a difficult situation.

The same could not be said for the other guests. Matthew smiled as he greeted his supper companions with nods, making his way to the one remaining empty chair at the table. Lord and Lady Gossling were doing their best to maintain their composure, but Lord Gossling was pale, and Lady Gossling had turned the particular shade of green that Matthew had come to understand meant seasickness. He would never forget that shade of green. Mr. Vernon and his wife were similarly pale, and young Phillip Vernon gripped the table with both hands as the ship pitched once again.

Lady Sudbury let out a distressed moan at the motion, grasping the table as well. Matthew had just taken a seat by the woman's side and instinctively grasped her hand.

"Do not worry, Lady Sudbury," he told the woman with a smile. "If the movements of the sea distress you, you may grasp onto my hand for stability and support."

Matthew didn't expect much, but Lady Sudbury surprised him by sending him a grateful, if weak, smile. She didn't seem capable of following that up with words, but she tightened her grip around Matthew's hand.

"It isn't as bad as all that," Matthew went on as the captain had a word with the crewman who Matthew assumed would be serving their supper, along with Miss Kingston. Both nodded, then set to work bringing several covered dishes to the table. "See?" Matthew told Lady Sudbury while watching Miss Kingston. "Miss Kingston isn't unsettled by the coming storm at all. She is a pillar of efficiency and calm, don't you think?"

His smile expanded when Miss Kingston glanced briefly at him. His admiration for her grew at the way she continued with the task she was given without flinching. He'd made a promise to advance her cause with Lady Sudbury in every way he could, and he was happy to do so, even under the current circumstances. Lady Sudbury seemed to have a higher opinion of Miss Kingston than she had of him.

"I do not know what all the fuss is about," Captain Mercer said as he took his seat at the head of the table and reached for his wine glass. Its wine splashed around as he lifted it. "I've weathered much worse storms than this. Mark my word, this will be but a memory by the time the sun rises on the morrow."

He held his glass aloft for a moment, then somehow managed to drink it without spilling a drop on his fine clothes.

All of Captain Mercer's guests hesitated before attempting to raise their own glasses in toast. A few of them did attempt the gesture, but apparently it took a bit of practice to be able to drink while a ship rolled and pitched around them. Matthew had just had his jacket laundered, thanks again to Miss Kingston, and he wasn't about to risk staining it all over again by sipping wine, even if the alcohol would have been just what he needed at that moment.

"How long do these storms usually last?" Lord Gossling asked, his face wan with barely concealed fright.

Captain Mercer shrugged. "A day at the most. Perhaps two, if it is truly bad. This isn't a hurricane, mind you. If we'd had so much as a hint of a hurricane on the horizon, we never would have set out from Jamaica."

"But one does not always know when a hurricane is on the horizon. Is that not true, Captain Mercer?" Mr. Vernon asked, doing his best to converse as Miss Kingston and the crewman served what might have been a fine supper of ham, potatoes, and vegetables on any other occasion.

"There are signs to watch out for," Captain Mercer said, cutting into his ham as though they were in the middle of a stable continent instead of bobbing on the ocean.

An explanation of maritime weather prediction followed as food was served. Matthew couldn't truly call it a conversation, because the captain was the only one who seemed capable of any sort of discourse at all. He went on about wind patterns and observations of tides and currents that went entirely over Matthew's head.

Matthew was too busy attempting to work out how he could eat some of the small feast placed before him with his stomach tying itself in tighter and tighter knots to listen to explanations of the intensity of previous storms Captain Mercer had sailed through. He took small bites and swallowed carefully, determined to eat the vegetables, at least, since he knew they would be a rare commodity in a few more days.

He was one of the few people at the table who made any sort of attempt to eat. Most of the ladies were near tears as they stared at their plates. Mrs. Collier had even raised a lace-edged handkerchief to her mouth and looked as though she was on the verge of casting up her accounts entirely.

Of everyone in the cabin, it was Miss Kingston who appeared most determined to weather the storm, both literally and figuratively. The clever woman had obviously seen that little or none of the food she was serving would be consumed. She served the smallest portions imaginable, then tidied up the rest, taking the sight and scent of it as far from the queasy guests as she could. Captain Mercer might have been oblivious to the distress of his supper guests, but Matthew had the feeling Miss Kingston thought of nothing else.

When a clap of thunder sounded far too close to them for Matthew's comfort, he set down his fork and said, "Captain Mercer, forgive me for interrupting, but might it not be wise to see your guests back to their cabins for the duration of the storm?"

Most of Matthew's fellow guests looked relieved at the suggestion. Mrs. Vernon burst into tears and nodded vigorously.

Captain Mercer sighed. "It is nothing, I tell you. It will all be over soon."

"That is what I am afraid of," Lord Gossling said in a dire voice.

Matthew couldn't help but search out Miss Kingston and send her a knowing grin at the comment. It was not kind to find humor in the distress of others, but the entire situation had taken such a turn for the ridiculous that Matthew couldn't help but laugh at it.

A moment later, even he was not laughing as a flash of lightning seen through the cabin's small windows was followed by a loud peal of thunder.

"We truly should return to our cabins," Matthew insisted, appealing to the captain with a look.

"Very well," Captain Mercer said. "If you insist."

"We do," Lord Gossling said, rising so quickly he knocked his chair backwards.

The motion of the ship didn't help the gesture. In fact, at that moment, the ship rolled again, sending both Lord Gossling and the chair flying.

Several shouts and whimpers rose up as the supper guests struggled to their feet, suddenly in a panic.

"There is nothing to be concerned about," Captain Mercer insisted. "It is not even that bad."

He was ignored soundly. Phillip Vernon was the closest to the cabin door, and as he threw it open, a lashing of rain spattered him from the deck above.

"Oh, dear," Lady Sudbury gasped, flinging her arm out and catching Matthew's hand. "I fear I might faint."

"I have you, Lady Sudbury," Miss Kingston said, leaping to the countess's rescue.

Matthew couldn't have been prouder of her. Miss Kingston was able to do so much more than he could as the two of them helped the countess to scoot her chair back, then to stand. It would have been entirely improper for Matthew to lay a hand on Lady Sudbury's person, but Miss Kingston was able to wrap her arm around the woman's waist and all but carry her to the door as the guests departed.

The entire landscape—if it could even be called that at sea—had changed by the time Matthew, Miss Kingston, and Lady Sudbury made their way to the steps leading up to the deck. The sun had set entirely, bathing the upper deck in darkness. The only light to guide them across the middeck came from lanterns that dangled from the rigging or that were affixed to the masts.

Fortunately, the crew must have known the captain's guests would need assistance returning to their cabins. Some enterprising soul had strung a thick rope across the deck for the guests to grab hold of so that they would not lose their footing or be thrown into the ocean with the rolling of the sea.

"Grab hold of the rope, my lady," Miss Kingston instructed Lady Sudbury as the woman wobbled her way up the stairs. "Lord Westbrook will go in front of us, and I will follow closely behind. You will be completely sheltered in every way."

"Yes, yes, please," Lady Sudbury said, her voice wavering. "Please help me."

"I will, ma'am," Miss Kingston promised her as Matthew stepped ahead of them, right into the lashing rain, to grab hold of the rope.

"Oh! It is raining so hard," Lady Sudbury lamented. "I shall be soaked."

"Do not worry, Lady Sudbury, I have you," Miss Kingston insisted.

She ducked back into the captain's cabin for the briefest of moments, returning with one of the pewter plates they had eaten off of. Even though the gesture was completely ridiculous, she held the plate above Lady Sudbury's head, as though it was an impermeable shield.

Part of Matthew wanted to laugh, but the rest of him marveled over the fact that it actually worked. Lady Sudbury seemed to summon the courage to follow him up onto the deck, and as long as Miss Kingston followed close behind, holding the plate over her head, she continued across the wild, windy, stormy deck.

It took far longer than it ever should have to cross the deck completely. For a few moments, as Matthew caught glimpses of the swelling waves as illuminated by lightning, he was tempted to think the situation was dire. He'd never been in a storm at sea, and he found it to be an experience he never wanted to repeat.

Now and again, he glanced over his shoulder, gripping their guide rope tightly as he did, to ascertain Miss Kingston's situation. Each time, he found her staring determinedly ahead, one arm holding the plate above Lady Sudbury, the other clasped firmly around the rope. Miss Kingston's single-minded determination gave him the courage to go on.

Finally, after what felt like forever, they reached the far side of the deck and descended to the corridor of passenger cabins. Lady Sudbury burst into tears and threw herself into Miss Kingston's open arms. Matthew smiled, grateful that that part of the ordeal was over, and deeply pleased for Miss Kingston. Surely, after the trauma of that night, the countess would see fit to hire Miss Kingston to be the most trusted of housekeepers.

"Your cabin is just here, Lady Sudbury," Miss Kingston

told the woman as she walked her to the door. "You'll be safe inside until the storm has passed."

Hard on the heels of those comforting words, twin cries of, "Uncle Matthew, Uncle Matthew! We're going to be swallowed up by the sea!" sounded from the end of the corridor.

"Don't you worry," Matthew said, nudging past where Miss Kingston had just deposited Lady Sudbury by the door to her cabin so that he could rush to his nieces and scoop them into his arms. "It's just a trifling storm," he said in imitation of Captain Mercer as he crouched so they could hug him tightly. "It will all be over soon."

He picked them both up, one in each arm, and started carrying them to their cabin at the end of the hall, across from his, but they shrieked and writhed in his arms.

"Miss Kingston!" Helly shouted, reaching out behind him.

"Miss Kingston!" Hibby echoed. "We cannot forget Miss Kingston."

Matthew twisted to glance over his shoulder. Miss Kingston was in the process of handing Lady Sudbury off to Dora. At the girls' cries, she looked to them. For a moment, indecision lined her pretty face. Matthew could practically see her fighting to choose between the girls who adored her, but to whom she only owed temporary loyalty, and the countess who could provide her with everything she'd dreamed of for her future.

It took only a moment for her to decide.

"Dora will take care of you, my lady," she said, letting go of the countess, then starting down the hall toward Matthew and the girls. "My charges need me now."

Matthew smiled, despite the storm and the chaos and the twins' fear. As Miss Kingston strode down the hall toward them, he couldn't help but think that perhaps she had not just chosen the girls, perhaps she had chosen him.

CHAPTER 6

She had done an admirable job of hiding her fear, if Kyria did say so herself. She'd seen at once both that the storm would be worse than any of them had previously thought, or than Captain Mercer had promised, and that the guests in the captain's quarters needed her to remain as calm and unflappable as possible.

That didn't mean she wasn't a roiling ball of terror on the inside.

"Miss Kingston! Miss Kingston!" Hibiscus cried out, extending her arms so that the only natural course of action was for her to grasp the girl and take her from Lord Westbrook's arms when she drew near him.

The action, combined with another deep roll of the ship, caused her to stumble to the side. She was saved by her proximity to the corridor wall, but her shoulder was smashed against it to the point of bruising.

"Are you all right, Miss Kingston?" Lord Westbrook asked at once, his face a study in control. Kyria could see the rising panic in his eyes, though.

Seeing Lord Westbrook alarmed was all that Kyria

needed to swallow her own fear and to continue pretending that she as a bulwark of strength.

"I am well, my lord," she said, now having to shout over the roar of the waves against the ship's hull, the crashes of thunder that sounded all around them, and the creak and groan of the ship itself as it rocked. "Perhaps we should settle the girls in bed for the night."

Lord Westbrook looked a bit startled at the pedestrian suggestion at first. He then seemed to grasp the importance of pretending as much as possible for the sake of the twins.

"You are right, Miss Kingston," he said. "Bedtime is in order."

The two of them took the girls into the cabin Kyria had been sharing with her charges since the voyage began. The small room was in complete disarray, due to the storm. The shelves and cupboards were constructed to contain items in spite of the rocking of the ship, but the storm was too much. Half the bed linens had fallen off the bed that the girls were sharing, one of the cupboards containing toiletries and other essential supplies had burst open and scattered its contents across the floor, and the pitcher that went with the wash-basin in the corner had fallen and its handle had broken off.

All of the spilled things continued to roll and fly across the floor as the ship pitched, making it all the more difficult to walk across the room.

"We're going to sink, we're going to die," Heliconia sobbed as Lord Westbrook reached the bed, then was forced to sit heavily on it as the motion of the ship threw him.

"No, we're not," Lord Westbrook told her, as though the notion were ridiculous. He glanced to Kyria with a wary look all the same, though.

"There is no need to worry, my darlings," Kyria said, sitting on the bed by Lord Westbrook's side, Hibiscus still clutching her neck so tightly Kyria was afraid she'd be suffocated. She returned Lord Westbrook's wary look, but the moment of intense communication only inspired her to set the man at ease. "Captain Mercer just told us that storms are a small thing to endure at sea. He said he has sailed through much worse than this with barely a scratch. Isn't that right, Lord Westbrook?"

Lord Westbrook had watched her speak with wide eyes, his thoughts clearly elsewhere, likely focused on the fear he felt. He shook himself and said, "That is absolutely right. It only seems dire and dangerous to us because this is the first storm we've sailed through."

"I do not like it," Heliconia said, her voice muffled as she buried her face against her uncle's neck. "Make it go away."

"I fear I cannot make it go away," Lord Westbrook said, worry making him pale.

Kyria knew there must be a better way to reassure children than to tell them there was nothing to be done. "I can make it go away," she said, feigning utter confidence.

Both girls lifted their heads from where they had been hiding and stared at her. Lord Westbrook seemed just as taken with the notion that she had power over the sea as well.

"We can all make it go away," Kyria said, "by singing to it."

"Singing to the sea?" Hibby asked, blinking, her lashes wet with frightened tears.

"Yes," Kyria insisted. "The sea is only trying to frighten us, you see," she went on, inventing her story as she went. "If we show it we are not at all frightened, then it will grow tired of frightening us and become calm again."

"An excellent idea, Miss Kingston," Lord Westbrook said with a relieved smile. "I know a few country songs myself. Do you know The Barley Mow?"

Kyria nearly laughed at Lord Westbrook's choice of a

drinking song. It was better than a staid hymn, though, and as it turned out, she did know it.

She nodded, and Lord Westbrook started off with, "Here's good luck to the pint pot, good luck to the barley mow!"

Somehow, singing seemed to work to calm the girls. They didn't know half the songs that Lord Westbrook launched into with enthusiasm. Kyria didn't know all of them either. Every one sounded as if he'd learned them in a local pub or festival somewhere in the country or at university. They were cheerful and easy to learn, though, so in no time she was singing along with him.

Within an hour, even though the storm continued to toss them about and lightning continued to flash around them, the girls dropped off to sleep. That was an even greater miracle than the parting of the Red Sea, as far as Kyria was concerned. It also meant that, without the girls in need of a steadying presence to calm them, Kyria could let her own anxieties show.

"Miss Kingston, are you quite alright?" Lord Westbrook asked once they'd stood and tucked the twins into their narrow bed.

Kyria tried to smile reassuringly at him, but the ship gave a particularly fierce lurch at that moment, nearly knocking her over.

"No, I am not," she confessed in a slight wail. "I'm terrified. What if the girls are right and Captain Mercer is wrong? What if this is more than a simple storm? It has been ongoing for hours and hours, and I am beginning to think it will never end. What if we all die?"

Of all things, Lord Westbrook laughed. Kyria snapped to face him with a furious scowl, but he said, "And here I thought I was the only one afraid for my life."

Somehow, that made everything better. "You have so

59

much to live for, my lord," she said, forcing herself to stand as straight as she could with the ship bobbing.

Lord Westbrook laughed again. "I have so many responsibilities to fulfill, you mean," he said. "I've the girls, for one. I don't know where they would go or what would happen to them without me."

"You truly care for them, do you not?" she asked. It seemed a bizarre and far too intimate topic of conversation for the moment, but the world had been turned on its head anyhow, and as far as Kyria was concerned, there was no guarantee that she would live to see another day.

That feeling was underscored by a bright flash and a particularly loud clap of thunder, and that was followed by a crack somewhere on the deck above. The ship rolled right after, and despite her attempts to maintain her balance, Kyria was thrown forward.

Lord Westbrook caught her, wrapping his strong arms around her and holding her close. Kyria ignored every rule of propriety that had ever been drilled into her and threw her arms around him, holding him tightly. She felt so much better with his large, strong body in her arms, surrounding her, that she was tempted to weep.

"I do care for them," he said, a tightness to his voice that indicated he was speaking to calm his nerves. "They are nearly all I have left in the world after George's and Henry's deaths. Well, there are my sister, Elizabeth's children, but I rarely see them."

Kyria nodded against his shoulder to let him know she'd heard him.

The ship dipped with particular ferocity, and the two of them nearly fell over onto the girls as they somehow managed to sleep on.

"We should not be standing," Lord Westbrook said, searching around. His gaze eventually fell on the door.

"Would you mind terribly returning to my cabin so that we can sit on the bed there? We can keep the doors open in case the girls awake."

Kyria nodded, then pulled herself together enough to stand. "A wise idea."

They extracted themselves from each other and stumbled out to the hallway, fighting to maintain their footing as the ship was tossed, and then into Lord Westbrook's cabin.

Lord Westbrook's cabin was tidier than the girls'. He had either secured his belongings better or he had fewer of them in the first place. Either way, Kyria and Lord Westbrook made their way to the narrow bed with as much ease as possible, then flopped gracelessly onto it. Kyria had to admit that despite the impropriety of huddling on a bed with an earl, it felt much easier to weather the storm when she did not need to exert effort to remain upright.

"And what about you, Miss Kingston?" Lord Westbrook asked as he clasped his arms around her once more. "What things do you care about in this life?"

Kyria's brain took a moment to catch up to his question. The sea banged against the hull, men shouted elsewhere on the ship, and thunder continued to rumble around them, and here was Lord Westbrook, asking her about what she loved.

"I do love my father," she blurted without thinking of the consequences. "He can be a gruff man, but he is fair and considerate. He could have tossed me out when I was born, or when my mother died, but he did not. He kept me, and he has always loved me and wished the best for me."

Lord Westbrook hummed—Kyria could not hear the sound, but she felt it in the vibrations of his chest—and said nothing. The fact that he did not ask who her father was told her he already knew. Anyone who had spent the last few months living at Spring Garden with them would have known simply by watching Kyria and her father interact, or seeing the resemblance between them.

"I did not want to leave my home to travel to England," she went on, since they were speaking with complete honesty and she had no secrets left. "I wished to spend my life running my father's household, but he wishes to marry a woman he has been corresponding with, and he says he wishes better for me than to endure that woman's scrutiny."

"That must seem very unfair to you," Lord Westbrook said.

Kyria straightened as much as she could and looked straight at him. They were in extremely close proximity because of the storm, but she felt as though he were emotionally close to her in that moment as well. He understood.

"Yes," she said. "It is unfair. Particularly as everything happened so swiftly. Father says I will be able to find a better life in England, a better position in a grander household, Lady Sudbury's household, if I'm lucky. But to me, it feels as though I've been cast out. And now this." She looked around at the swaying, bobbing cabin, then clutched Lord West-brook tighter.

"I cannot say I know your feelings precisely, Miss Kingston," Lord Westbrook said, "but I, too, was cast out from the life I thought I would live and forced to assume another role entirely."

"And what did you want before, my lord?" Kyria asked.

"To go into medicine of some sort," he said. "I've been fascinated with healing and surgery. As a younger son, I could have made something of that, but not now."

"I am sorry you could not pursue your dream, my lord," Kyria said.

"Please call me Matthew," he said, then immediately

looked startled by his own boldness. "I mean...well...perhaps that is not appropriate?"

"I will call you whatever you'd like, my lord, Matthew," Kyria laughed—mostly because of hysterics from the odd situation they found themselves in. "I have yet to be convinced we will make it through the night, so there will be no one to chastise us for gross informality in the morning."

"If this is our last night on earth, Miss Kingston," Lord Westbrook, Matthew, said, "then I am glad to be spending it with you."

He stared intently into her eyes, and suddenly Kyria put a name to the kindness and the warmth he'd always shown her. He did not just care for the twins, he cared for her as well. Perhaps he had from the very beginning, when they were still mostly strangers occupying the same space in her father's house, but with minimal interaction. The two of them had certainly become friends on the voyage so far. Perhaps there was something more?

"Call me Kyria," she said, though the fury of the storm around them made her words sound small and muffled.

Matthew seemed to hear them, though. "Kyria," he repeated her name, smiling at her as though their lives weren't in immediate peril.

And then he did the most incomprehensible thing Kyria had ever known a man to do. He pulled her in tight and slanted his mouth over hers, kissing her with abandon.

The storm raged, the ship dipped and rocked, and the wind and sea howled and battered all around them, but everything within Kyria seemed to calm with that kiss. She was already in Matthew's embrace, but she clung to him even tighter, threading her fingers through his hair and kissing him back with a passion she didn't know she possessed. Matthew was the kindest, sweetest, and strongest man she'd ever known. Nothing else mattered but the safety she felt in his arms.

Any notion she might have had that he would kiss her once and be done with it was dashed to pieces—like she felt the ship might be at any moment—when he shifted to kiss her again. His hands caressed the curves of her body beneath the soaked fabric of her dress, and she warmed to his touch at once.

She wasn't certain what made her do it, other than the feeling that this might be her one and only chance to be wicked in the very short remainder of her life, but she fumbled for the buttons of his jacket, then his waistcoat, as she continued to kiss him and sigh into his mouth. The sounds they both made were swallowed by the storm entirely, but that only encouraged Kyria to grasp for more.

Matthew was, evidently, of a mind with her. He rolled her to lie across the bed, then reached for the soggy hem of her gown, tugging it up over her stockinged leg. She knew she should have stopped him. She should have demanded that he show some forbearance, or at least shut the cabin door. But neither of them seemed capable of doing anything more than what they were doing. Kyria continued to push at his clothing, peeling it back as much as she was able, then reaching for the falls of his breeches.

The whole thing was madness in so many ways, but once the passion began, Kyria couldn't stop herself. She tugged Matthew's shirt up and pushed his breeches down as much as she could so that she could play her hands along the bare, damp flesh of his hips and belly. He had a firm, flat, well-muscled torso that she never would have guessed at, considering the fit of his clothes. Even more exciting than that, her hands brushed across the stiff spear of his erection as it sprung free of its confinement. He was long and girthy, and even though she had never handled a man's member before, she'd seen enough through happenstance to know Matthew had nothing to be ashamed of.

Matthew stopped kissing her with a groan as she stroked him with trembling hands. "I've no wish to lead you into anything you do not want," he managed to growl out, clearly overcome with pleasure. "But I want you more than I've ever wanted any woman in my life right now, and if I go to a watery grave without having you, well, I think it would be disappointing for us both."

Kyria couldn't help but smile at his honest way of putting it. Her heart beat as though it would burst from her chest, but not merely with fear of a possible, imminent death.

"Yes," she said, wriggling and helping him pull at her skirts. "Yes, I want you as well," she panted, spreading her legs as best she could in the confining bed.

Matthew made a wild sound that could very well be laughter, but the roar of the sea drowned it out. His kiss was just as expressive when he slanted his mouth over hers again while wriggling between her legs and lifting her thighs with his strong arms so he could position himself just so. He hesitated for a moment, lifting his head to gaze down at her, questions in his eyes.

Kyria gripped the back of his neck and arched her hips in an attempt to bring that part of him that had only just made contact with her most intimate place closer to him, but in that moment, the ship dipped sharply again, which caused Matthew to practically fall into her.

They both gasped and groaned as the motion of the ship pushed Matthew past her body's momentary resistance. The feeling of fullness and excitement that followed was far better than Kyria had been led to believe the moment would be. There was a certain madness in it as well, as if the sea had taken her virginity as well as Matthew.

Either way, all caution was thrown to the howling wind

after that. Matthew continued to thrust into her with enthusiasm, and Kyria met those thrusts with a determination to enjoy the scandalous moment to the fullest. She did not care that the cabin door was still open or that thunder still cracked around them. She wanted Matthew, and she wanted to give him all of herself.

Her body responded in kind by coiling tighter and tighter, then bursting with pleasure when it all became too much. She cried out, certain the storm carried the sound away, and clutched Matthew for all she was worth. Matthew responded by thrusting harder, his own cries growing louder. When he tensed from head to toe and continued to thrust a few more times before groaning and sagging over her, Kyria knew that neither of them would ever be the same again.

She was too spent in the wake of what they'd done to do more than wrap herself around Matthew as best she could as the ship continued to bob and creak and shudder. None of it mattered anymore, though. If this truly was to be the last night of Kyria's life, it was the best, and it was worth it.

CHAPTER 7

They were not going to die. That thought hit Matthew with a hint of sheepishness deep into the earliest hours of morning, when the storm abated and the ship ceased to rock violently. It also occurred to him that there were consequences to not dying the same as there would have been to death as he held a sleeping Kyria in his arms long after the shocking liberties he'd taken with her.

He had behaved with shameless impulsivity the night before. The temporary belief that they were both staring death in the eye was no excuse. He had taken advantage of Kyria in a moment of high emotion, and for that he felt…bad?

The fact of the matter was that he did not feel bad. Not at all. Granted, he wished he'd had the ability to take more time and to truly savor Kyria. He wished he'd been able to ensure that she enjoyed herself as much as he had. They'd both been so frantic, though, and neither of them had been thinking straight.

Which was why he carefully extracted himself from Kyria's sleeping embrace when the sounds of activity aboard the ship hinted that they were in danger of imminent discovery. Kyria deserved to sleep on after the bravery she'd shown in getting everyone through the storm while she had been frightened herself. The unflappable calm she'd been able to show, while inwardly being afraid, only made Matthew admire her more.

He considered it a roaring success that he was able to leave the bed without waking her. His first order of business after he did was to tip-toe across the corridor to check on his nieces. They had apparently slept soundly through the waning storm, which was a testament to how exhausted they'd been. But as soon as Matthew stepped through the doorway into their cabin, they groaned and stretched awake.

"Is it over?" Helly asked, rubbing her eyes.

"Is the ocean quiet again?" Hibby asked as she sat up.

"The storm has passed," Matthew assured them, moving to sit on the bed so that the girls could hug him as they dragged themselves the rest of the way out of sleep. "You see? There was nothing to worry about in the end after all."

Perhaps there wasn't anything to worry about with the storm, but as Matthew hugged the girls and kissed their tousled heads, he glanced across the hall to Kyria sleeping in his bed. He was anxious that he had a great deal to worry about, once the clear light of day struck.

"Shall we tidy up this room so that Miss Kingston is not burdened with the chore once she awakes?" Matthew asked the girls, standing and bringing them with him.

They managed to pick up most of the things that had fallen out of cupboards or rolled off the table before Kyria awoke. The rest of the ship seemed to be waking as well. As morning sunlight filtered in through the portholes, a veritable symphony of sounds rose up all around them. People were walking around the decks above them once more, and other passengers' voices could be heard through the walls.

Matthew swallowed, glancing at the wall dividing the twins' room from its neighbor. He and Kyria had made quite a bit of noise in the throes of passion the night before. They'd been fortunate that the storm had been even louder than them. The storm was enough to hide or excuse everything they'd done, but Matthew still felt uncomfortable with the whole thing.

Kyria woke not long after they started tidying. She rose and did her best to straighten her appearance, though Matthew was certain that even a woman as fastidious about her appearance as Kyria was would be excused from looking a bit worse for wear on that particular morning.

All the same, Matthew's heart beat faster and his whole body flushed with heat as Kyria slowly made her way from his cabin to the girls'. When she met his eyes with a look that said their lovemaking was fresh in her mind and her feelings about it were as jumbled as his, Matthew's heart squeezed hard as well as beat faster.

She truly was the loveliest woman he'd ever met. How outrageous would it be, really, if he transferred his intentions to her? She was the daughter of a marquess, after all, and even though—

"Miss Kingston!" Helly shouted, dropping the things she'd been picking up and flying to her governess. "Miss Kingston, I was so worried!"

"I was worried too!" Hibby cried, rushing to throw her arms around Kyria as Helly did.

"We've made it through the storm," Kyria said, smiling at the girls. "And you both look none the worse for wear."

"It was terrifying," Helly rushed on as Kyria stepped fully into the room, bringing the girls with them.

She met Matthew's eyes with a soft look of question, as if she wanted him to tell her that things would work out after all and that they were still friends. Perhaps she wanted more.

"The sea was frightening," Hibby said, gazing up at Kyria with haunted eyes. "I thought we were all going to drown."

"But you made it better," Helly said, almost as if Kyria had not been in the thick of everything the girls were describing. "You made the angry sea go away."

Kyria laughed, dragging her gaze away from Matthew and giving her attention to the girls. "I'm certain you played your parts as well. Are we cleaning up now?" she asked, seeming to shake off every other implication from the night before. "Let me help."

That was the end of that. The mood had shifted, and all of the unanswered questions Matthew had—did Kyria hate him? Had she enjoyed their congress? Would it happen again? And perhaps even did she feel more for him now?—went unanswered.

They finished putting the twins' cabin to right as much as possible, though much of it was still damp and the bedding and some clothing needed to be aired to dry completely. Matthew headed abovedeck to assess the situation on the ship while Kyria and the girls strung clothesline through both cabins.

As far as Matthew could tell from what he saw above, they had been extraordinarily lucky. The masts still seemed to be intact, though one of the yardarms had cracked or been struck by lightning. It hung at an odd angle above them, held aloft by the rigging only. There were already sailors repairing it, and a few other bits of the ship that had been cracked or broken. The deck was littered with debris, but even that did not appear as bad as it could have been.

"You see?" Captain Mercer said, striding over to him from near the main mast, where he appeared to be directing the cleaning efforts. "It was just an ordinary storm. Nothing to worry yourself overmuch about."

Matthew arched one eyebrow at the man. His idea of

nothing much was everyone else on the ship's brush with death.

"Do your men need help setting the ship to rights?" he asked, glancing around.

"Not from an earl, my lord," Captain Mercer told him with a sly look.

Matthew helped out regardless, even if that help was merely moving barrels out of the way of the crew who were engaged in repairs and directing a few of his fellow passengers who had come up to the deck away from the men who were working.

He had just begun to share stories of making it through the storm with Phillip Vernon when Lady Sudbury climbed up onto the deck with her maid in tow.

"Oh, Lord Westbrook," Lady Sudbury exclaimed, pressing a hand to her chest at the sight of Matthew. "Thank heavens you are here and that you have survived our ordeal in one piece."

"I managed, Lady Sudbury," Matthew said with a bright smile. He would not have managed without Kyria, though. Even without their moment of passion—if those words were, indeed, adequate enough to explain the way he'd felt with Kyria—Kyria's strength and quick thinking had made a terrifying evening easier to bear.

"We all managed, thanks to you, Lord Westbrook," Lady Sudbury went on, rushing closer to him. Poor Dora had a difficult time keeping up, especially as she had a parasol that she attempted to keep above Lady Sudbury so that it shaded her from the morning sun. "If not for you, I am quite certain none of us would have survived."

Matthew blinked in surprise at the compliment. "I played but a small part in getting everyone to safety," he said with a modest bow of his head. "The ship's crew acted with exemplary care to help us all across the deck and to our cabins, and it was Miss Kingston who was of particular help to you."

"But it was you who had the quickness of mind and calmness of demeanor to carry us all through, my lord," Lady Sudbury insisted. "You carried me through."

There was a light of interest in the woman's eyes that had not been there the night before. Matthew was alarmed by it, particularly when Lady Sudbury inched closer to him and gazed fondly at him.

It was only when her gaze dropped to the level of his chest that he realized he hadn't changed into fresh clothing from the night before. Indeed, while he still wore his jacket and waistcoat, neither were buttoned, and his neckcloth was untied. For all intents and purposes, Lady Sudbury was staring at him in his shirtsleeves. That she liked what she saw was a bit alarming.

"I did what needed to be done," Matthew said, flushing hot under the woman's scrutiny. "Any man would have done the same."

"Oh, no. You were a hero, Lord Westbrook," Lady Sudbury insisted. "Do you not think he was a hero, Mr. Vernon?" she asked young Phillip.

"I suppose so," Phillip said. "I was too intent on saving my own life to take much notice."

"Lord Westbrook was, indeed, a hero," Lady Sudbury went on.

Out of the corner of his eye, Matthew spotted Kyria climbing onto the deck with Hibby and Helly. All three had changed into clean dresses and had smoothed back their hair. A rush of tenderness hit Matthew at the sight of them.

"Miss Kingston was the true hero," he said, speaking loud enough to catch Kyria's attention and to draw her over. "She was the one who selflessly assisted you back to your cabin."

"Yes, I suppose so," Lady Sudbury said. She glanced

briefly to Kyria, though the look in her eyes wasn't half as appreciative as Matthew thought it should have been. "I believe it is you to whom I owe my thanks above all else, Lord Westbrook. Would you be so kind as to escort me on a turn about the ship so that I might enjoy the air? The storm has left things frightfully damp below."

Matthew nearly choked on his own tongue. There was no possible way Lady Sudbury's words could have been meant lasciviously, but the way the widow suddenly seemed interested in him, and the way she clutched his arm and batted her eyelashes at him, left him feeling decidedly awkward.

There was nothing for it but to take Lady Sudbury on a short promenade around the ship, although he was able to rush back to his cabin to set his appearance to right first. Lady Sudbury was correct to say that everything was soggy after the storm, and that the sunshine was a welcome relief. It was not as though the woman could attempt anything inappropriate as the two of them strolled in plain view of the rest of the crew and passengers—many of whom had come up to dry out as well—especially with Dora trailing along, doing her best to protect her mistress from the sun.

Matthew found that he would rather have been anywhere else than with the woman he was meant to be courting, though. And even that was not true. As he and Lady Sudbury reached the aft deck and glanced out over the activity and repairs underway on the rest of the ship, his attention was caught by Kyria and his nieces as they walked around the foredeck. Kyria was doing a good job of keeping the restless girls occupied by pointing to the sailors in the rigging as they repaired ropes and sails.

Matthew had almost forgotten Lady Sudbury was on his arm entirely when she said, "The Westbrook estate is near Dartmouth, is it not?"

"Er, Exeter," Matthew said, bending to the side a little so

that he could keep Kyria and the girls in his sight as they climbed down from the foredeck and moved across the middeck.

"And you have a house in Mayfair?"

Matthew almost didn't hear the question. Kyria appeared to be coming closer, which made his heart speed up.

Several beats too late, he answered, "My brother has a house there. Had. Has. I suppose it is my house now. I've yet to see it, though."

"You haven't been to London?" Lady Sudbury blinked rapidly in shock.

"Oh, no, I've been to London many a time," Matthew answered, shifting his attention fully to Lady Sudbury as Kyria and the girls mounted the stairs to the aft deck. "My parents kept a house in Fitzrovia, but George sold it to purchase the Mayfair house upon their deaths."

"I assume that is where you intend to live when you are in town?" Lady Sudbury asked.

"Uncle Matthew, there are men in the ringing!" Hibby announced, breaking away from Kyria and racing to him. Helly was close behind her.

Matthew's attention was demanded in two places, but choosing between them was the easiest thing in the world.

"I believe it's called rigging, not ringing, love," he said, holding out his arms so his nieces could give him quick hugs...and ignoring Lady Sudbury's question entirely as he did.

Lady Sudbury made a small sound that might have been disapproval, Matthew wasn't paying attention.

"I am terribly sorry," Kyria said with an uncharacteristically bashful look as she approached them. Uncharacteristic, but beautiful all the same. The sunshine did wonders for her appearance. Or perhaps it was the secret sparkle in her eyes as she glanced to Matthew.

Either way, he felt as though the deck were wobbling under him again.

"The girls insisted on coming here to tell you all their observations," Kyria went on.

"Children should be kept silent and maintained in their own sphere," Lady Sudbury said, wrinkling her nose. "They are an unwanted disturbance in most cases."

"That is what Miss Benning always used to say," Helly said with a dramatic sigh.

Matthew snorted before he could stop himself. He pressed a hand to his mouth momentarily, then said, "Sorry." He cleared his throat and went on with, "The men are in the rigging repairing the damage from last night."

Before either of the girls could comment on that, Lady Sudbury said, "Miss Kingston, would you be so kind as to fetch me a cup of tea? I believe that young man is serving it to the other passengers, and tea would settle my nerves."

Matthew was irate with Lady Sudbury's order for all of half a second before Kyria smiled graciously at the woman and said, "Of course, Lady Sudbury. You need only ask, and I will obey."

All at once, Matthew remembered Kyria's intentions toward the countess. He remembered what she'd said about her future in the height of the storm as well. Kyria had wanted to run her father's household, and apparently Quintrell had told her she could do much better in England. Lady Sudbury was that much better. Kyria depended on impressing the countess to win herself a place once they arrived in England.

And he'd pledged to help her in that endeavor.

As Kyria turned to go, Lady Sudbury called, "You can take the children with you on your errand," as though asking Kyria to remove a pair of fish carcasses.

"Yes, of course, my lady," Kyria said with a gracious nod

of her head. "Come along, Lady Heliconia, Lady Hibiscus. Would you like some tea as well?"

"And biscuits?" Helly asked, rushing after her.

"I want biscuits too," Hibby said.

Matthew watched the three of them descend to the middeck, where one of the younger crewman did, indeed, have a tray with cups of tea that he offered to the harried guests as they came up from below.

"You would do well to hire a different governess for those girls once you reach London, my lord," Lady Sudbury said, shaking Matthew out of his thoughts as he watched Kyria and the twins approaching the lad with the tea.

He registered the statement a beat too late—again—and turned to the countess. "I beg your pardon?"

Lady Sudbury wrinkled her nose. "I worry that she is not dedicated enough to her position," she said.

Matthew had never heard anything so ridiculous. Kyria made a perfectly splendid governess.

But that wasn't the future she wanted for herself. Kyria wanted something entirely different, and it was within Matthew's power to help her to that.

"She has ambitions of being a housekeeper," he told Lady Sudbury. "She was more or less a housekeeper at Spring Garden before agreeing to be my nieces' governess for the voyage. I believe she wishes to find work as a housekeeper in England, so if you know of anyone who is searching—"

"I do not," Lady Sudbury cut off the end of his thought. She turned straight to him with a smile and said, "But perhaps I could provide you with the names of a few experienced governesses once we reach home. A hero such as yourself should have only the best England has to offer in your employ." She went so far as to rest a hand on his arm.

Matthew stared at her hand, perplexed. Had he truly made so much of an impression on the countess through what he considered very ordinary and necessary actions during the night before? Was Lady Sudbury impressed by his disheveled appearance at last, or perhaps by what she had spotted under his clothes? It baffled him that a woman could change her mind so quickly, and that she might see him as a viable suitor now.

Then again, he supposed that coming close to death, as he had certainly been convinced he was for a moment the night before, caused one to make decisions about their future happiness.

He glanced down to the middeck just as Kyria turned toward him. She smiled when their eyes met, and Matthew's heart seemed to grow in his chest. He had made decisions in the intensity of the storm as well, but were those choices truly viable? It was outrageous for an earl—even a newly made, horribly inexperienced one—to consider a woman like Kyria for his future happiness. Even if he was certain she was the perfect mate for him. But could he truly travel that path? Or should he abandon fancy and dream to do what was expected of him and continue with his suit toward Lady Sudbury? He simply did not know.

CHAPTER 8

$\mathcal{T}$he storm might have been over, but as the *Anthem* sailed on through the Atlantic, Kyria continued to feel as though the ground were shifting beneath her feet. She had done something deeply scandalous with Matthew—and the fact that she could only think of him as Matthew now and not Lord Westbrook as she should have, was telling. The trouble was, she did not regret her actions, not for one moment.

No, the true problem Kyria faced over the next days and weeks of the voyage was that Matthew would not speak of what they'd done.

She was certain his silence was not out of any sort of regret or embarrassment. The way Matthew gazed at her as she sat on the foredeck, giving the twins their daily lesson, or the way he always seemed to be aware of her as they went about their monotonous daily business on the ship was as sure a sign as any that he had at least some of the same tender feelings toward her as she had for him.

But every time they came close to speaking of the matter, every instance where they might have professed feelings for each other, was interrupted by either Lady Hibiscus and Lady Heliconia in need of one sort of attention or another, or by their fellow passengers, who all seemed to live piled on top of each other as the novelty of the voyage wore off and everyone sought activities or conversations to occupy themselves.

Even at night, it was impossible for Kyria and Matthew to do more than glance wistfully at each other across the hallway after the girls had gone to bed before one of the other gentlemen passengers coaxed Matthew into a game of whist, or any of the ladies' maids accompanying their employers asked for her advice on how to mend a tattered hem or how to fend off sea sickness.

At least those inquiries from the ladies' maids served to establish Kyria as the wisest and most competent of assistants aboard the *Anthem*.

"However shall I climb down a ladder such as that in this gown, Miss Kingston?" Lady Sudbury asked when the *Anthem* reached the islands of the Azores many weeks into the journey. "I am desperate to set foot on dry land, but to require me to climb down a rope ladder like a monkey so I can be conveyed ashore in a boat?"

Kyria kept a serene smile on her face, even though she was close to boxing Lady Sudbury's ears for being difficult.

"It is your choice, my lady," she said with as much cheer in her voice as she could feign. "You could remain aboard the ship while the crew replenishes the supplies."

"No! I want to go on the land!" Heliconia shouted, as if Kyria had made the suggestion to her and not to Lady Sudbury.

Lady Sudbury stared at the twins with her lip curled. Nearly four weeks of being in close quarters with the girls and she had not warmed to them one bit.

"Allow me to escort you, Lady Sudbury," Matthew said,

stepping in to rescue the situation. "Neither Miss Kingston nor I will allow any harm to come to you as you make your way into the boat."

Lady Sudbury turned to Matthew with a flush on her otherwise sallow cheeks, blinking rapidly. "Do you think so, Lord Westbrook?"

Matthew glanced to Kyria with a look of wistful fondness that she was coming to know a bit too well. He then glanced back to Lady Sudbury and said, "You are in the very best of hands."

"Well, if you insist, Lord Westbrook," Lady Sudbury said, inching to the edge of the railing, where several of the *Anthem's* crewmen were helping passengers climb down to the boats below.

"Allow me to precede you down the ladder," Kyria said, moving ahead of Lady Sudbury. "That way, I will be able to direct your steps, assist you into the boat itself, and preserve your modesty in the process."

Lady Sudbury gasped and pressed a hand to her chest, as though she had just recognized the threat to her modesty. "You are too kind, Miss Kingston," she said in a haunted voice.

It took a bit more convincing from there, most of which happened while Kyria balanced on the rope ladder, halfway down to the bobbing boat, as Lady Sudbury hesitated. Kyria wished she'd seen how the countess had boarded the *Anthem* in the first place. She imagined a series of pulleys and perhaps a secure box were involved.

Matthew coaxed Lady Sudbury into descending the ladder in the end, and as Kyria made certain the countess was settled, he himself climbed down with the twins clinging to him like monkeys.

From there, they were rowed into the port city of Ponta Delgada, where the process of shuffling Lady Sudbury out of the boat proved to be as irksome as getting her in had been. The countess fussed and complained, poor Dora nearly burst into tears as she struggled to keep a parasol over her mistress's head, and it was all Kyria could do to reassure the woman that she would enjoy her excursion, if she simply allowed herself to.

Kyria was overjoyed once they were all finally on land, and once Mrs. Vernon and Lady Gossling—who had been conveyed ashore in one of the other boats—whisked Lady Sudbury away to see what the shops of Ponta Delgada had to offer.

"Lord Westbrook, are you coming with us?" Lord Gossling called out to Matthew from a group of the grandest of the male passengers as they started off in the opposite direction from the ladies.

Matthew glanced to them, his mouth open, as if he might tell them no, then at Kyria. The same longing and helpless fondness she'd seen from him since the storm was bright in his eyes. Kyria held her breath, praying that he would choose to spend the day with her and the girls as they made a historical tour through the city as part of their lessons.

But in the end, Matthew let out a breath, his shoulders dropping, and called to the men, "I will be with you shortly." He glanced back to Kyria and the girls—who were severely disappointed—and said, "You understand, I trust. I have appearances to keep up, and Lord Gossling is a good model for how I should behave now as a peer."

"I understand completely, my lord," Kyria said with a reassuring smile. "You must attend your friends. Your nieces and I will never be far away."

"We are on an island," Hibiscus said. "There are not many places we can go."

Kyria grinned at her charge's wit and charm. "Your niece

is correct, my lord," she said, grinning at Matthew again. "We will never be far from you."

Matthew smiled back at her as though she'd whispered endearments to him. He then touched the brim of his hat, then turned to walk off and join the other men.

"I wish Uncle Matthew would stay with us," Heliconia said with a disappointed sigh, taking Kyria's hand as she offered it.

"So do I, my dear," Kyria told her, taking Hibiscus's hand as well. "So do I."

Her moment of disappointment was brightened as she and the girls set off on their exploration of the city. Porta Delgada was quaint and beautiful with white, stone buildings that shone in the sun, and pretty gardens planted with colorful flowers. Kyria didn't know if it was her relief at being able to walk for more than a few yards without confinement or the clear, crisp day, but the island reminded her somewhat of home. The flora and fauna were different, but the same sense of isolation against the sea and verdant possibility from the countryside and low mountains in the distance filled Kyria with a sense of the familiar.

That only made her homesick though. And it reminded her that she had yet to fulfill her purpose for taking the voyage.

"The city has been inhabited since fourteen-forty-four," Kyria recited to the girls from the small guidebook they had purchased from a stall near the harbor as they wandered through the central shopping thoroughfare. "After an earthquake in fifteen-twenty-two devastated many of the other settlements of the islands and the capital at the time, Ponta Delgado became the administrative seat of the—"

"Look over there!" Hibiscus interrupted her, clearly not interested in island history.

"It's a bird!" Heliconia shouted in turn before both girls dashed off to chase the colorful creature.

Kyria sighed, shut her guidebook, and raced after the girls as fast as she dared while in company.

As it happened, the girls dashed right past Lady Sudbury and the other gentlewomen from the *Anthem*. They nearly knocked Dora off her feet in the process. Dora dropped Lady Sudbury's parasol, and as Kyria was near enough to go after it, she lunged forward until she caught the thing.

At the same time, she saw that the twins had moved on to another object of fascination and called out, "Lady Hibiscus, Lady Heliconia, come back!"

"I will fetch them," Dora said, perhaps a bit too eagerly. She sent Lady Sudbury a scathing look over her shoulder, then dashed after the girls.

Kyria was left to step in by holding the parasol above Lady Sudbury's head. Rather than seeing the moment as a chore, however, she grasped the opportunity in front of her.

"Thank you, Miss Kingston," Lady Sudbury said, her smile tight.

"It is my pleasure, my lady," Kyria said. Her heart sped up and she took the chance in front of her to add, "I would quite like to serve you more, once we reach England."

"Oh?" Lady Sudbury asked, peeking anxiously to the other ladies as they walked on ahead, gazing through the window into a shop.

"Yes, Lady Sudbury." Kyria drew in a breath, summoned all her courage, and said, "I have trained extensively as a housekeeper. I am proficient with numbers and accounting, and with running a grand house. It is my hope that, once we reach England, I will be able to gain employment in a large, settled house. Your house, perhaps?"

She fought not to wince at her boldness, smiling hopefully at Lady Sudbury instead.

"I see," Lady Sudbury said, her manner not at all encouraging. "Well, I am certain that you have a great deal of expertise at being a house…servant." The way she stumbled over the last word sent prickles down Kyria's back. Had the woman been about to suggest she'd been enslaved?

"I have been a free woman from birth, Lady Sudbury," she said, hoping that it would be the one and only time she would need to state as much openly.

"Oh? Oh. I see." Lady Sudbury cleared her throat nervously, then attempted to smile once more. "Your skills have been evident on the voyage, Miss Kingston," she went on. "I will give the matter of your employment some thought. Now, if you will excuse me." She hesitantly took her parasol from Kyria, shading herself. "I must rejoin my friends."

Kyria had never been dismissed with so much false kindness in her life. She stood where she was for a moment after Lady Sudbury walked away, feeling as though all her hopes for the future she wanted had just been dashed.

She could not dwell on it, though. She had responsibilities to fulfill.

And yet, when she turned to search for the girls, she found them playing in a nearby fountain, attended by Dora. Dora appeared happy for the first time since Kyria had met her. She clearly liked the girls, and they seemed to get along with her. The three of them splashed in the fountain, laughing and enjoying each other's company.

Kyria could not, in good conscience, steal Dora's one moment of happiness from her by sending her back to a mistress she evidently did not like. And as long as the girls were accompanied, she felt no need to rush to them. Which left her standing where she was, at more than a bit of a loss.

At least, until a short hiss sounded from the garden just to her right.

Kyria turned her head to find Matthew half concealed

behind a large shrub, gesturing to her. Immediately, her heart lifted, and far more joy than she had any right to feel enveloped her.

She rushed straight to Matthew, ducking into the garden with him. "Are you not investigating the city with your friends?" she asked as Matthew cupped her elbow and drew her deeper into the garden.

"They wish only to investigate Ponta Delgada's pubs, which I do not have a taste for," he said. "I would rather take this blessed opportunity to have a moment with you."

Kyria's heart fluttered to her throat. It was everything she'd wanted since the storm, but did not believe she could have. The garden seemed to be the perfect setting for their assignation—if it could even be called that—as well. Great urns planted with flowers of every color stood around them. A trellis arched over a small bench that seemed perfect for lovers enjoying each other's company. The greens of the garden were bright and cheery, and they made a spectacular contrast with the white of the buildings and the deep blue of the sky.

"I have thought on this matter for quite some time," Matthew began, rubbing the back of his neck nervously, though there was a smile in his eyes, "and I am not certain what to say or how to proceed."

"Say what you must," Kyria told him. "I will not be offended if you wish to speak candidly."

In fact, she hoped that he would spill out all of the emotion that was clear in his eyes and that he would declare himself. She wanted to sink into his arms and pledge her life-long devotion to him. But she maintained as serene a manner as she could, standing straight with her shoulders back, her hands clasped demurely in front of her.

"About the storm," Matthew began, even more nervous than before. "I…I took liberties, but I…." He blew out a heavy breath, inching closer to her. "I haven't been able to think of anything since. As wild and irrational as my actions were, I do not regret them for a moment."

"Neither do I," Kyria said, her voice higher than it should have been. "I have thought back to the night of the storm with fondness myself."

She cursed herself for her stilted words. She should simply tell him that nothing in the world had ever felt as wonderful as the two of them joined, and if he wanted her, she was his.

But how, and in what capacity? Matthew was an earl. She was not suitable for him. He had his sights set on Lady Sudbury, in a manner of speaking, and she was unequivocally the better match for him.

Except that she could see in every part of him the regard he had for her, and he radiated deep affection for her. If ever there were a man who might go against public expectation and defy the rules of his class and the *ton* to secure his own happiness and hers, it was Matthew.

He seemed to feel at least some of what her thoughts suggested. His smile softened, and he reached for the bush beside them to pluck a bright and colorful bloom.

"Kyria, you must allow me to—"

"Lord Westbrook, here you are." Lady Sudbury's voice broke the moment of blissful expectation as certainly as if a cannonball had been launched into the garden. "I've been searching everywhere for you."

Not only was the statement patently false, the smile Lady Sudbury wore as she marched into the garden was grating. She did not spare a single glance for Kyria as she swept her way right up to Matthew, forcing him to turn away from Kyria to address her.

"Lady Sudbury," Matthew said with a polite bow. "Are you not accompanying the other ladies on their excursion?"

"I find that I am not enamored of shopping at the moment, Lord Westbrook," she said, batting her eyelashes at him. "Perhaps you could find something else I might be enamored of?"

Kyria clenched her jaw and just barely stopped herself from making fists as well. How dare Lady Sudbury interrupt the moment she had waited weeks for?

But of course she would dare. Lady Sudbury was a countess, Matthew was an earl, and in Lady Sudbury's eyes, Kyria was a servant. Not even a servant, she was a woman of mixed race applying to be a servant.

"What is that in your hand, Lord Westbrook?" Lady Sudbury continued with her flirting.

"This?" Matthew blinked at the flower, as though he wasn't entirely certain how it had gotten there. "Oh, I suppose it is a flower." He glanced past Lady Sudbury to Kyria with a look of apology and longing.

"It is very lovely, my lord. Thank you," Lady Sudbury said, plucking the flower from Matthew's hand.

Kyria's spirits deflated entirely with the gesture. It was symbolic of so many things. She was a fool to think that she could capture the love and attention of a man like Matthew. He could be as fond of her as he liked, and she in return, but their positions in life were too different. She had been wrong to consider herself anything more than a governess to him.

Without a single word, she turned and started out of the garden.

"Miss Kingston," Matthew called after her, a sense of urgency in his voice.

"Let the poor woman go and collect her charges," Lady Sudbury scolded him. "Someone needs to mind those little creatures. Now, tell me what you know of this garden we find ourselves in. It is quite secluded, is it not?"

"Allow me to escort you back to the square, my lady,"

Matthew said, following Kyria, though she didn't turn around to look at him. "We wouldn't want to be caught in a garden without chaperonage, would we?"

A chill shot down Kyria's back. It would indeed be horrific if Matthew and Lady Sudbury had been discovered alone in the garden. It was patently unfair that the same could not be said for her. Because as much as she adored and longed for Matthew, even being caught in a compromised position with him would not be enough to clear the way for the two of them to be together. The most she could hope for where Matthew was concerned was to be in his employ for the length of the voyage.

It was time for her to face the truth that whatever warm feelings she had for Matthew, it would all be over soon.

CHAPTER 9

*E*ngland was fast approaching, and Matthew did not know what to do. Captain Mercer had informed him that they would reach Southampton in less than a week, but he had yet to decide whether to succumb to the demands of his new title and ask for Lady Sudbury's hand…or whether he should throw every bit of caution he had to the wind by telling Kyria how much he adored her.

His adoration had only grown on the last leg of the voyage, since their conversation in the garden in Ponta Delgado. He had wanted to curse to high heaven at the way they'd been so rudely interrupted, and just when he'd thought they might have come to some sort of an understanding.

Kyria had looked radiant in the morning sunlight, framed by bright blossoms and verdant greenery. He'd been able to see the hope and the longing in her eyes. She'd whispered to him that she had welcomed his lovemaking during the storm —well, she'd told him she thought of that night with fondness, and his imagination had elaborated the details of that confession in the nights since then. But he knew in his heart of hearts that his elaborations were what Kyria would have said if she'd been given the chance.

But now, there they were, plodding along in a grey sea, the skies overcast and dull above them, a nip in the air that said they would reach their final destination soon, and the cold light of duty and responsibility seemed to follow Matthew's every step.

"Are you going to do it, man?" Lord Gossling asked as the entire ship prepared for an evening of dancing on the decks that Captain Mercer had devised to boost his passengers' spirits. "Are you going to declare yourself to your lady love?"

Matthew swallowed hard at the question. He schooled his features into a smile and faced his fellow peer. "I have yet to decide," he said, feeling rather sick as he spoke.

Lord Gossling laughed, clearly misunderstanding the crux of Matthew's indecision. As far as the viscount was concerned, he probably thought Matthew was caught between wanting to propose to Lady Sudbury on the ship or waiting until they made land.

But that was the least of Matthew's worries. His choice was one between doing exactly what was expected of him as an earl or doing what his heart truly wanted. The former was safe. The latter would end with him banished from all polite society, and very likely Kyria, the twins, and any children he and Kyria might have in the future as well.

And yet, he knew they could all be happy as society's outcasts. He would be, at least. He'd never intended to be part of society to begin with, and he would have been perfectly content to keep to Exeter and the family's country estate for the remainder of his days, never so much as glancing in London's direction. But was that what Kyria wanted? Was that what was best for George's girls?

"Lord Westbrook, you look as though you've eaten a spoiled prawn," Lady Sudbury said, approaching him as he and Gossling watched the preparations for the evening's activities.

Matthew turned to her with a weak smile. "I am well, Lady Sudbury," he said. "I am simply anxious to get on with things."

Gossling snorted beside him. "I would wager you are," he said, then thumped Matthew's shoulder hard enough to sent him off-balance. "Do excuse me, Lady Sudbury," Gossling went on with a sly glint in his eyes. "I believe I'm needed elsewhere."

Matthew sighed and watched the man go, then turned to Lady Sudbury, bracing himself for whatever topic she wished to converse about.

"I am quite looking forward to this dance tonight," she said, smiling prettily. "It feels as though it could be the culmination of the voyage, as if a great many things might come to pass tonight. Do you not think so, Lord Westbrook?"

She inched closer to him, which was too close, as far as Matthew was concerned. The indifference she had shown him at the beginning of the voyage had vanished after the storm. Whether it was his supposed heroism or the fact that Kyria had kept his wardrobe tidy and instructed him in courtly manners and deportment, or whether Lady Sudbury had set her sights on him simply because there were no other unattached gentlemen aboard the *Anthem*, Matthew would never know.

Except, there was one way to find out.

"Lady Sudbury, if I might ask," he began. "What about me do you find so interesting? Why have you given me so much of your attention?"

Lady Sudbury blinked rapidly and recoiled a bit, as though he'd slapped her with the question. "Why should I not find you to be the most amiable and pleasing of men, Lord Westbrook?" she asked.

"But do you?" Matthew asked on, turning to face her fully. "Do you truly find me so grand?"

Lady Sudbury's smile widened. "Certainly. Particularly after your heroism during the storm. And, as Lady Gossling has reminded me, a man of your character who has newly inherited his title must be in want of guidance."

Strangely enough, her answer made him relax. So the title was her aim after all. And chances were that Lady Gossling had encouraged her into pursuing him.

Matthew glanced out across the deck to where Kyria and the girls were helping with decorations for the evening. Perhaps his choice was not so difficult after all. Lady Sudbury's interest in him was of a sort that would diminish after the voyage, he was certain. He could not help but feel as though Kyria's regard was of a sort that would last for years to come.

But that did not change the circumstances of both potential matches.

"Miss Kingston, would you be so kind as to help me with my gown for tonight?" Mrs. Collier asked, striding across the deck toward Kyria.

Kyria turned to her, which required the risky action of taking her eyes off the twins. "I would be delighted to, Mrs. Collier, but my charges require my attention."

"I'll watch them," Matthew called out without hesitation. He turned to Lady Sudbury long enough to say, "Please excuse me, my lady," then, without waiting for an answer, he nodded to her and crossed the deck to Kyria.

Their eyes met, and Kyria blossomed into a grateful smile.

That smile was cut short far too soon as Kyria darted a look to Mrs. Collier, then schooled her expression to neutrality.

"I will mind the girls while you help Mrs. Collier,"

Matthew said, saving Kyria from any embarrassment at being caught smiling at him.

Kyria smiled at him once more, pausing simply to look at him for a bit too long, then said, "Thank you, my lord."

She curtsied slightly, then gave Matthew one last, lingering glance before heading off across the deck with Mrs. Collier.

"It is the salt air and water," Mrs. Collier said, speaking as though Kyria were an inferior. "It has caused havoc with the delicate muslin of my gowns."

Matthew couldn't help the uneasy feeling that stayed with him as Kyria disappeared below deck. His heart felt as though it had been sewn into the lining of her bodice so that she might carry it around with her wherever she went, but could she truly? The risk to her would be even greater than the risk to himself if he declared himself, and he had no wish to hurt such a remarkable woman that way.

"Uncle Matthew, look at this," Helly called to him from near the mainmast, where she and Hibby were helping one of the crewmen hang lanterns.

Matthew turned to his nieces, ready to make a comment on whatever they were doing, but at the sight of the two girls working diligently to hand streamers made of rope and bits of cloth, inspiration struck.

"Girls, might I have a word with you?" he asked, striding over to them.

The twins glanced to each other as though they had never heard such a ridiculous request.

"Would you care to take a turn about the decks with me?" he asked instead.

"Yes, please," Hibby said, dropping her decorations at once and skipping over to him.

Helly followed with the same amount of enthusiasm. It warmed Matthew's heart, and he took their hands in each of his. There were so many things he regretted about his brother's death—the situation George's demise had landed him in, the loss of a brother and friend, the difficulties of managing the finances his brother had left behind—but the chance to become a friend and guardian to his nieces was something Matthew would forever be grateful for.

And as those nieces would be directly affected by whatever decision he made, it was only right to consult with them before making up his mind.

"I have a matter of greatest importance I would like to discuss with the both of you," he said, helping them up the stairs to the aft deck, which was the least populated by fellow passengers at that moment.

"I am quite good with things of importance," Helly informed him, her chin tilted up at a jaunty angle.

"I like to help," Hibby said with a sweet smile.

Matthew's heart felt as though it were too large for his chest. It was not just Kyria who had changed his life, the twins had added to it immeasurably as well.

He walked them all the way to the back railing, where they were able to look out at the wake the ship left behind.

"Girls," he began in a serious voice, "I find myself faced with a choice that will alter all of our lives forever."

Helly suddenly looked terrified. "You aren't going away and leaving us, are you, Uncle Matthew?"

"Please do not put us in an orphanage," Hibby nearly shouted, hugging his arm tight.

"Whoever said I would put you in an orphanage?" Matthew asked, horrified at the suggestion. "You are my girls now."

Both twins looked immensely relieved.

"Lady Gossling told Lady Sudbury that when the two of you marry, she can send us away to a school," Hibby said.

"Which is the same as an orphanage for ladies, is it not?" Helly asked.

"No," Matthew said with a frown. "It is not the same thing, precisely. And you need not worry, because I have no intention of sending you away from me."

The twins hugged him, and Matthew rather liked it.

There were other things he did not like, though.

"When did Lady Gossling say this to Lady Sudbury?" he asked.

"A week ago?" Helly said, looking confused.

"I do not know what day it is anymore," Hibby confessed.

Matthew broke into a smile. He had lost track of the days himself. Time seemed to move at a different pace at sea.

"Now that we have that out of the way," Matthew said, "I should very much like your opinions. I have not determined whether I should marry Lady Sudbury or not, but—"

"Please don't marry her, Uncle Matthew," Helly said with utmost seriousness.

"I do not like her," Hibby added in a whisper, her face pinking, as if she knew she shouldn't be speaking out against her elders.

Matthew fought against the notion that those opinions alone were enough to make his decision. He owed it to himself to be more rational in his decision-making, though.

"There are things you may not have considered," he said, crouching so that he was at their eye level. "Do you wish to be accepted into society when you are older, to have your coming outs, and to attend balls and parties?"

"Like our dance tonight?" Hibby asked, her face lighting up.

That was another sort of answer that Matthew could not ignore. His nieces were lively, social creatures, even at their young age. He could imagine them being even more so once they were older.

"Something like that, but in London," he said. "If I married Lady Sudbury, you would be accepted into society, and you might even be named diamonds of the first water, or whatever it is that young ladies seek to be called these days."

"I like diamonds," Hibby said, blushing even more.

Matthew laughed. If that was what she took from his words, then so be it.

"The other choice," he went on, "is to live a quiet life in the country, away from society, and to perhaps not be accepted by the grand people of London."

"I've never been to London," Helly said with a shrug. "Papa always said it was a big, smelly, vile city."

Matthew's eyes went wide. The twins had rarely spoken of their father since they'd set out from Jamaica. He hadn't thought to ask whether that was because the grief of losing him was too raw and too big, or because they'd had too many other things to occupy them.

But now, as he thought of it, he imagined what George would say about the predicament he found himself in now. Would George have approved of his attentions to Kyria? George was an abolitionist, as Matthew himself was. He had always spoken of the people of Jamaica as if they were entitled to his respect. George could easily have taken the twins back to England and deposited them with their sister, Elizabeth, but he had chosen to raise them in the Caribbean. That seemed to indicate that the *ton* was not George's first consideration in his plans for Hibby's and Helly's futures.

"What do you think of Miss Kingston?" he asked the girls in a quiet voice. He had to fight not to smile too much or give any indication about what he felt for Kyria, lest it influence their decision.

But both girls smiled right away and grew visibly excited.

"Miss Kingston is wonderful," Helly said. "She taught us all about pirates and naval battles of the recent war."

"And she gave me books and taught me to read much faster than Miss Benning ever did," Hibby added.

"She is ever so pretty," Helly added. "And she said that I am pretty too."

"And she never mistakes us for each other," Hibby said, glancing to her twin. "Miss Benning mistook the two of us all the time."

Matthew laughed. He never would have considered that an asset, but for twins as identical as Hibby and Helly, he could see it was of great importance.

"So, what would you think if I married her?" he asked in a rush, before he could lose his nerve.

The girls gasped, their faces filling with surprise and delight.

"Yes, Uncle Matthew!"

"Oh, yes, please!" They shouted at the same time.

"Can I ask her for you?" Helly asked.

"No, I want to," Hibby said.

Matthew laughed. His mind was all but made up. "It is only right and proper that I should ask her," he said, standing straight and resting his hands on the girls' heads. "But since I know how difficult it is for you to keep secrets—and this is a secret for now—I will ask her at the dance tonight so that none of us have to wait long."

He would have asked her straight away regardless, but there was too much activity on the ship at present, and he wanted the moment to be romantic.

"Is that what you wished to discuss with us?" Helly asked.

"Who you should marry?" Hibby followed.

"That is it," Matthew said, holding his hands wide to show he had nothing else to hide.

"Definitely Miss Kingston," Helly said.

"Not Lady Sudbury," Hibby added, her eyes wide with horror.

It was settled, and as far as Matthew was concerned, the girls had made a good choice.

He took their hands again and led them back to the main deck and their previous decorating activities. They surprised him by keeping his secret. Or perhaps it was their renewed interest in the decorations that kept them from blurting out the discussion to everyone within sight.

Matthew felt a contentment that he hadn't known was possible as he stood back near the door to the lower decks to watch them. They would all have a fine and happy life together. He didn't need to be at the center of London society to be happy, and he suspected the rest of his surprising family wouldn't either.

"Lord Westbrook, I fear you slipped away from me earlier before I could fully answer your questions," Lady Sudbury said, walking up beside him, as though she'd been waiting for him to come back so that she could pounce.

"My questions, my lady?" he asked, blinking at her.

"Yes," Lady Sudbury said, beaming at him. She did more than that, she grasped his arm with both hands and sidled close to him. "What I find so interesting about you is your boundless good cheer and your determination to make those around you happy. And I wish to do the same for you. I will make you unendingly happy, Lord Westbrook. For I cannot imagine anyone I would rather spend the rest of my earthly days with than you. We will be so happy together. So, to answer your other question, yes. Yes, I will marry you."

Matthew blinked in surprise, the bottom dropping out of his stomach. "I did not—"

He wasn't able to finish his statement before a gasp sounded from a few feet below. With a feeling of dread, he turned to find Kyria just about to climb up from the lower decks. Her eyes were wide with shock, which was proof enough that she had heard everything Lady Sudbury had just said.

"Kyria," Matthew called to her, shaking out of Lady Sudbury's grip.

But before he could fully extract himself, Lady Sudbury clamped down on his arm, and Kyria dashed back into the corridor, disappearing into the shadows.

CHAPTER 10

K yria's heart didn't just break, it shattered when she heard Lady Sudbury accept Matthew's proposal. She was a fool for daring to hope. Matthew had a duty and a responsibility to his class. He could never consider her.

But she had given her heart away, and it was too late to shield herself from the pain of the truth.

She had nowhere to go as she ran away from the stairs leading abovedeck, nowhere but the far end of the corridor. But the memories that surfaced as she neared Matthew's cabin were too much for her. She turned to flee in the other direction, but the ship's walls seemed to close in around her. She was trapped in a heartbreak of her own making.

Before she had a chance to decide what to do, Dora pulled open the door to Lady Sudbury's room, poking her head into the corridor to see what was the matter. When she saw Kyria, her eyes went round.

"Miss Kingston," she said, stepping into the hall and wringing her small hands together. "Are you well? Has something happened? Not another storm, I hope."

Kyria pressed a hand to her mouth to stop a wail from escaping and shook her head.

Dora glanced toward the stairs, then made her way over to Kyria. "Has some evil befallen Lady Hibiscus and Lady Heliconia?" she asked.

Kyria shook her head again, then summoned her courage. She dropped her hand, drew in a breath, squeezed her eyes shut, then said, "Lady Sudbury has accepted Lord Westbrook's proposal."

Kyria was not certain what she expected in response to her revelation, but it was not silence. The rest of the ship seemed to carry on with various thumping and calls, she could even hear sea birds above, but nothing else.

Slowly, she opened her eyes to find Dora looking thoroughly perplexed. When Dora caught her expression, all the young maid said was, "That is curious."

Kyria's heart quivered with unlikely hope in her breast. "What could be curious about it?" she asked. "Lord Westbrook is an earl and the finest man I have ever known. He is in want of a wife of good character and breeding. And Lady Sudbury is a countess and in want of a husband."

"She is that," Dora said. "But she was certain she had lost her chance at winning Lord Westbrook."

Kyria frowned. "Why would she think that?"

Dora's gaze seemed to focus. She pressed her lips together, glanced over her shoulder at the hatch leading abovedeck, then took Kyria's arm and walked her the full length of the corridor, to where they would not be disturbed.

"Lady Sudbury believes Lord Westbrook has discovered her secret," Dora said.

"Her secret?" Kyria blinked rapidly.

Dora nodded. "Before she married Lord Sudbury, my mistress was no better than I am."

"I beg your pardon?" Kyria was even more befuddled.

"Lady Sudbury was the daughter of one of Lord Sudbury's tenants, Miss Kingston," Dora continued in a whisper. "Lord Sudbury fell in love with her and married her, even though it caused a scandal in the county. That's why he took her away to Jamaica. No one there knew of my mistress's origins, so they could not dismiss her and shun her for her low birth."

"But surely word of her origins would have reached Jamaica," Kyria said. "The island is remote, but we still hear the gossip from England there."

"That is what my mistress fears," Dora said. "That is why she kept her distance from the likes of Lord Westbrook at first. She was certain he would have heard the story of her birth and that he would shun her for it."

"But he didn't know," Kyria said. "I'm not certain he would have shunned her to begin with. Matthew is good and kind and—" Kyria gasped and pressed her hand to her mouth when she realized she'd called Matthew by his given name.

Dora grinned slightly, as if she knew, but continued with her story. "The more my mistress came to know Lord West-brook, the more she realized she could be safe with him. She has no wish to give up the life to which she has become accustomed, you see, and since she failed to give Lord Sudbury an heir, Lord Sudbury's estate and title will pass to a brother. A brother who was scandalized by the match and who will most certainly turn the lady out."

"Oh, I see," Kyria said.

And she did see. Suddenly, she saw everything. Lady Sudbury stood on the precipice of complete ruin. She must have realized after the storm that all of her hopes for a comfortable future life lay in convincing Matthew to marry her before they reached England.

The woman had succeeded. She had secured a proposal

from Matthew, and now the two of them would marry. But what sort of scandal would the match expose Matthew to?

No more of a scandal than if Matthew had chosen her, Kyria realized with a pang in her heart.

"I didn't think Lord Westbrook would do it," Dora said, back to frowning in confusion once more.

"You did not?" Kyria asked, glancing mournfully at the young woman.

"No, ma'am." Dora shook her head. "Everyone aboard this ship, including my mistress, knows that Lord Westbrook is in love with you."

Kyria gasped. She hadn't realized they'd been that obvious.

But of course they had been. They had been utterly unable to hide their easiness with each other, or their stolen glances and smiles. They had been overly familiar with one another, though no one had taken them to task for it, and they had shepherded the twins together.

"I am surprised," Dora went on, frowning. "We all know that you are the much more suitable choice for Lord Westbrook."

"I am?" Kyria was confused once more.

Dora glanced to her with a cheeky grin. "There are no secrets aboard a ship, Miss Kingston," she said. "Everyone on the *Anthem* knows that you are Lord Quintrell's natural daughter."

"They do?" Kyria pressed a hand to her chest, feeling suddenly faint. She thought she'd hidden her secret well.

"Lady Gossling says you are the spitting image of him," Dora went on, smiling. "And Mrs. Collier pointed out that many a high-born man acknowledges and supports his natural children. Marries them off legitimately and all. Mrs. Collier and Mrs. Vernon have a wager between them as to which lady Lord Westbrook will choose, the natural daughter of a marquess who is pretending to be beneath her station, or the daughter of a tenant farmer who has gotten above herself."

Kyria could only blink at the characterization of the situation, completely at a loss.

Dora looked as though she would go on, but the clatter of footsteps on the stairs startled both women. A moment later, Matthew ducked into the corridor, looking exceedingly alarmed.

"Kyria, please let me explain," he said, marching boldly down the corridor to Kyria.

"I will leave you to it," Dora said with a giddy smile. She picked up her skirts and fled down the corridor, then up to the deck, sending Kyria a backward glance before she disappeared.

Kyria was left stunned and befuddled. She didn't even have the wherewithal to move as Matthew all but charged toward her.

"Please let me explain," Matthew said, coming to a stop in front of her. He was clearly agitated, as he could not stay still. "There has been a grievous misunderstanding."

"Are you engaged to Lady Sudbury?" Kyria asked, desperate to cut right to the heart of the matter.

"No!" Matthew said, blowing out a breath. Kyria thought he might have thrown his arms out to his sides as well, had there been room for it. "The blasted woman completely misunderstood the intent of a series of questions I asked her," he went on. "She took them as a marriage proposal when they most definitely were not."

"How did...did you...were there witnesses to these questions?" Kyria stammered. Her heart was beginning to crack and let in a great deal of joy over the turn things had taken, but there was still a chance that Matthew could be trapped into the marriage if the situation had been viewed in the wrong way by their fellow passengers.

"There were witnesses who agreed just now that my questions were not meant as an offer of marriage," Matthew said, his shoulders dropping as a great deal of tension left him. He even smiled. "A few of them went so far as to point out that I was quite obviously in love with another."

Kyria's face heated with self-consciousness, and a bit more of the joy she was trying so desperately to keep in check.

"They are right at that," Matthew went on, reaching for Kyria's hands. "I am in love with another. I am in love with you."

Kyria sucked in a breath, her eyes immediately stinging with tears of happiness.

Still grasping her hands, Matthew sank to one knee. "I love you, Kyria," he said, his voice laced with emotion. "This sea voyage has been fraught with every kind of adventure imaginable, but through it all, you have held your head high and taken charge of things. You have done wonders with the girls, and you have settled my own heart and mind on so many matters. I was terrified of everything that inheriting my family's title meant, but with you at my side, I feel as though I could face all of it and more.

"Not because I need you to be my teacher, mind you," he went on, his smile turning bashful for a moment, "but because I need you to be my love. You must admit, we are a good match of temperament and outlook. We both have marks against us, at least in the eyes of the *ton*, but I dare say neither of us particularly cares about society."

"I most certainly do not," Kyria said, her voice hoarse. "I only care about you," she admitted as the tears escaped from her eyes. "And about the girls."

"Yet another reason I love you," Matthew said, smiling up

at her fondly. "You love those girls as much as I do. They need you in their life as much as I do. Say you will be mine, that you will be ours. Say you will defy whatever social conventions say we should not be together to be mine regardless. Say you will marry me?" He lifted his eyebrows on the last statement, turning it into a question.

Kyria had no more doubts in her mind. "Yes," she said, squeezing Matthew's hands in hers. "Yes, of course I will be your wife. I love you, Matthew. I would love you whether you were a nobleman or a surgeon, or a simple farmer. You are the sweetest and most wonderful man I have ever met."

Matthew let out a sound of joyful excitement, then rose to his feet. He swept Kyria into his arms and kissed her with abandon. Kyria should have stopped him, since there was no such thing as privacy aboard a ship, but she found she did not want to. She kissed him back with equal passion, sighing loudly against his mouth.

Their moment of passion was broken by Heliconia saying, "You see? I told you so," from the stairs leading abovedeck.

Kyria gasped and pulled away from Matthew as he, too, turned toward the stairs. Heliconia and Hibiscus sat on the stairs, watching the scene with wide grins. Surprisingly, Mrs. Collier and Mrs. Vernon stood at the bottom of the stairs minding them.

"You owe me two guineas," Mrs. Collier told Mrs. Vernon with a sharp grin.

Mrs. Vernon sighed and shook her head. "Oh, very well."

"Are you and Miss Kingston going to marry?" Hibiscus said, breaking away from the stairs and racing toward Kyria and Matthew. Heliconia came with her.

Matthew glanced to Kyria, who he still held in his arms, with a wide smile, then said, "Yes. Yes, we are."

Hooray!" both girls shouted, jumping up and down.

"Can you marry her on the ship?" Heliconia asked.

"Mrs. Collier said that Captain Mercer can marry couples on the ship," Hibiscus added.

Matthew glanced to Kyria, his eyes bright with mischief and excitement. "What do you think?" he asked. "There is already a dance planned for this evening's activities. Shall we make it a wedding party?"

"That would be exceedingly unusual," Kyria said, breathless with love and giddiness.

Matthew laughed. "I daresay we two are exceedingly unusual, so it would be fitting."

Kyria beamed at him. "Then yes. I do wish to marry you aboard the ship, this evening, right now."

"I believe that can be arranged," Matthew said.

And arranged it was. Not a soul aboard the Anthem was surprised by the announcement that Matthew and Kyria would be married by Captain Mercer after supper that evening, just before the dance commenced. Kyria had never imagined marrying anyone, let alone an earl, and she most certainly had not imagined being wed by a ship's captain while out at sea.

The entire complement of the ship was eager to assist in every way, from decorating to helping Kyria to dress to providing musical accompaniment for the service. It was quick and simple all the same. Kyria and Matthew stood facing each other on the foredeck with the setting sun framing them as Captain Mercer read a few passages from the Bible, then performed the rites as Kyria and Matthew recited vows. It all happened in such a whirlwind that Kyria could hardly believe it happened at all, but as she and Matthew danced together under the light of the lanterns strung across the middeck, their friends and the crewmen wishing them every happiness, Kyria felt as though her heart was Matthew's forever, and his belonged to her.

The only person aboard who did not share in the sudden felicity of the evening was Lady Sudbury.

"What shall become of me now?" she lamented as she sat on a barrel weeping while the other passengers continued to dance. "I shall be cast off and end my days alone and unloved in some cottage on my deceased husband's land."

Kyria and Matthew exchanged a look, then Matthew said, "We would be happy to welcome you as a guest in our home, Lady Sudbury. Once we are established."

"Yes," Kyria said, feeling magnanimous toward everyone, after the turn her life had taken. "Come stay with us."

"It may not be precisely what you had envisioned for yourself, but I have quite a few friends who are not peers— surgeons and scholars and the like—who would not care at all where you came from or what your position in life is. You would like them, I think."

"Truly?" Lady Sudbury glanced up at Matthew as though he were her savior. "You would introduce me into such society?"

"Gladly," Matthew said.

Lady Sudbury blinked back tears. "Then I would be happy to be your guest, Lord Westbrook. And thank you."

Kyria felt a deep sense of satisfaction at being able to help the woman. She was not convinced Lady Sudbury would have done the same for her, but that was not a consideration for her. She wished only for the woman to be as settled in life as Kyria felt she would be now.

"You are a good man, Lord Westbrook," Kyria said, a bit of teasing in her voice, as she and Matthew retired to his cabin. Dora had agreed to watch over the twins for the night, and the rest of the passengers had hinted that they would stay abovedeck dancing, should Kyria and Matthew want a few moments alone.

"If I am a good man," Matthew said, sweeping Kyria into

his arms, "it is only by default." He laughed. "I truly do not know what I am doing."

"Perhaps not as an earl," Kyria said with a sly grin, already undoing the buttons of his jacket. "But as a husband, you are off to a magnificent start."

He laughed low in his throat, then leaned in to kiss her. Kyria gave herself over to the kiss, knowing that it was not only allowed, it was encouraged. She had spent the last several weeks since the storm wishing Matthew would kiss her again, and now the moment had come.

She finished with his jacket and pushed it from his shoulders, then started on the buttons of his waistcoat. Matthew kissed her ardently, tugging at the ties of her gown and pushing it from her shoulders once it was loosened.

"It is a shame we have only this tiny ship's bed for tonight," he murmured against her ear as they pulled at each other's clothing. "Wait until we are at Westbrook Hall in Exeter. The beds there are large and allow for a great deal of movement."

Kyria laughed, feeling decidedly wicked. "I cannot wait."

Neither of them could wait for that evening's consummation. They made as quick work of each other's clothing as they could, draping it all over the room's small chair rather than taking a care to hang it.

It was indeed a tight fit to tumble into the narrow bed, and the process of positioning themselves adequately caused a great deal of laughter. That laughter turned to sighs and moans of pleasure as Matthew lavished Kyria's breasts with kisses and stroked his hands over her sides and thighs.

"I have never been much of a lothario," Matthew confessed breathlessly as he worshiped her body with his hands and mouth. "Perhaps you could teach me that as well."

"Gladly," Kyria sighed, digging her fingertips into his shoulders and back.

As simple as it was, Kyria had never been happier with the way they twined their bodies together, exploring and enjoying each other to the fullest. It was worlds different from their frantic joining during the storm. They took their time, learning the taste of each other's skin and the sounds they both made as they gave and took pleasure. Kyria would have thought it would be embarrassing for a man to stroke her so intimately when she was in such a state, but the insistent press and slip of Matthew's hand and fingers against her sex was blissful beyond telling, and when her body burst into throbbing pleasure, she nearly sang with joy.

It was somehow even better when Matthew entered her with a long, tight groan. She could not remember if she'd experienced pain during the storm, when he'd done the same, but there was none now, only pleasure and a sense of souls entwining. She loved the abandon with which Matthew thrust into her, the sounds he made, and the way he seemed to come completely undone as he spilled his seed in her. It was complete perfection, because it was the two of them together.

"I love you, my darling Kyria," Matthew panted as they settled together, still entwined in the narrow bed. "I will give everything I have to make you the happiest woman alive."

"Then you have already succeeded," she told him, kissing him lightly and brushing his damp hair back from his brow. "For I am already happier than I have ever been. And I will dedicate my life to making certain the two of us live the very best of lives."

I HOPE YOU HAVE ENJOYED KYRIA AND MATTHEW'S STORY! THIS book is totally dedicated to the REAL Kyria, who I met on my first ever cruise aboard *Anthem of the Seas*. She was a member of the crew (and she actually knew who I was and had read my books!) and she was just so wonderful and friendly and awesome and took such great care of me, that I had to write this one for her. I hope I get to meet her again someday, maybe in her homeland of Jamaica!

IF YOU'RE LOOKING FOR MORE FUN AND STEAMY REGENCY romance from me, check out my series *When the Wallflowers were Wicked*, which begins with *The Accidental Mistress*. When your reputation is ruined, why not enjoy it? That's the philosophy Miss Verity Barnes and her sisters take after disaster befalls them at Almack's. Verity hatches the plan to become the mistress of a titled gentleman, and she sets her sights on the Marquess of Landsbury. But Verity has no idea what she's doing, and Thomas, Lord Landsbury, doesn't know what hit him when these two outrageous personalities meet! Find out what happens today with *The Accidental Mistress*!

IF YOU ENJOYED THIS BOOK AND WOULD LIKE TO HEAR MORE from me, please sign up for my newsletter! When you sign up, you'll get a free, full-length novella, *A Passionate Deception*. Victorian identity theft has never been so exciting in this story of hope, tricks, and starting over. Part of my West Meets East series, *A Passionate Deception* can be read as a stand-alone. Pick up your free copy today by signing up to receive my newsletter (which I only send out when I have a new release)!

Sign up here: http://eepurl.com/cbaVMH

. . .

ARE YOU ON SOCIAL MEDIA? I AM! COME AND JOIN THE FUN ON Facebook: http://www.facebook.com/merryfarmerreaders

I'M ALSO A HUGE FAN OF INSTAGRAM AND POST LOTS OF original content there: https://www.instagram.com/merryfarmer/

ONE LAST THING! DO YOU CRAVE HISTORICAL ROMANCE filled with passion and red-hot chemistry? Come join me and my author friends in the Facebook group, Historical Harlots, for exclusive giveaways, chat with amazing HistRom authors, raunchy shenanigans, and more!

HTTPS://WWW.FACEBOOK.COM/GROUPS/2102138599813601

ABOUT THE AUTHOR

I hope you have enjoyed *The Forty-Day Governess*. If you'd like to be the first to learn about when new books in the series come out and more, please sign up for my newsletter here: http://eepurl.com/cbaVMH And remember, Read it, Review it, Share it! For a complete list of works by Merry Farmer with links, please visit http://wp.me/P5ttjb-14F.

Merry Farmer is an award-winning novelist who lives in suburban Philadelphia with her cats, Torpedo, her grumpy old man, and Justine, her hyperactive new baby. She has been writing since she was ten years old and realized one day that she didn't have to wait for the teacher to assign a creative writing project to write something. It was the best day of her life. She then went on to earn not one but two degrees in History so that she would always have something to write about. Her books have reached the Top 100 at Amazon, iBooks, and Barnes & Noble, and have been named finalists in the prestigious RONE and Rom Com Reader's Crown awards.

ACKNOWLEDGMENTS

I owe a huge debt of gratitude to my awesome beta-readers, Caroline Lee and Jolene Stewart, for their suggestions and advice. And double thanks to Julie Tague, for being a truly excellent editor and to Cindy Jackson for being an awesome assistant!

Click here for a complete list of other works by Merry Farmer.

Printed in Great Britain
by Amazon